Coy Danewood

Rebuilding a Life

Book 2

PAUL ADAMS

Publishing Coordinator – Sharon Kizziah-Holmes

Paperback-Press
an imprint of A & S Publishing
A & S Holmes, Inc.

ISBN -13: 978-1-951772-44-4

DEDICATION

I want to dedicate this book to modern day ranchers. These days we live with iPhones computers, and computerized security systems, but to ranchers, cattle still have to be fed. Heifers need to be checked while calving. Big knot-headed bull calves still need to be pulled, especially on a cold stormy night. And mountain oysters, well, maybe we should just call them calf fries. To me, a pair of wood handled post hole diggers are instruments of torture, but they do get the job done. If none of this makes any sense to the reader, you should thank the next rancher you meet for providing those tasty steaks and hamburgers we all love.

Acknowledgments

First off, a big thank you goes to, Sharon Kizziah-Holmes, at Paperback Press. Sharon, I have really enjoyed working with you these past months. Even if you get together with my wife and gang up on me. Once again, I thank my editor, Ali Thompson, for all her hard work and thought-provoking questions. I want to thank, Jaycee DeLorenzo, for her artwork on the cover. I also want to thank my wife's sister, Shirley Hixson, for her proof reading. Ladies, thank you for all that you do. Sometimes you are a little tough on a guy, but I guess I needed it. Maybe, anyway, thank you all. ☺

Paul Adams

CHAPTER 1

Thinking Back

Sometimes when Coy was out feeding cattle by himself he would think back to the first time he saw them. Gunnar was only two. He and Judith looked so hopeless sitting there when the big man drove away and left them. He laughed when he remembered how defiant she was at first. Gunnar would have melted any man's heart he thought, climbing up and putting his little arm around a person's neck. He also remembered Judith coming to him after three years of marriage broken hearted.

"I just came from the doctor's office," she said. "He told me the STD that Frank gave me after Gunnar was born has made me sterile. It took me over two months to get it cleared up. Coy, I can't give you a child of your own."

He told her that day, and still felt the same, that he already had a family. He had a wife and child. That was six years ago. They had made it through their arguments about his early relationship with Darlene McDaniels and other problems. Judith was now a full-fledged rancher's wife. Gunnar was twelve and Coy was now teaching him how to be safe with a gun. Mostly they hunted rabbits down by the creek along the road. Gunnar could drive the pickup, the tractor and everything else on the ranch.

One day when Coy and Judith were walking back up to the house from the barn, he stopped and turned back towards the barn. Judith stopped and looked at him.

"Step back towards the barn and face me," he said. She just looked at him and didn't move. "I want to show you something," he said. She took two steps back and turned to face him. "Look up on the top of the ridge over my left shoulder and gently move back and forth," he said. She did then stopped rocking suddenly.

"What is it?" she asked looking up at the ridge to the east of their house.

"I'm going to point with my right hand down to the barn but never mind me doing it. I'm sure that reflection is Adam McDaniels watching what is going on down here."

"Why would he do that?"

"I'll tell you inside, let's just walk up to the house." Gunnar followed along behind them and they went in the house. Inside Coy told Gunnar to go sit on the front porch.

"Tell me why McDaniels is spying on us," she said.

He opened the door to make sure Gunnar was still sitting on the front porch, came back and sat down. He told her all of it, his parents' death, McDaniels urging the bank to force the sale of the ranch, and John Hull and Billy helping him. She shook her head.

"How big is his ranch?"

"Over 12,000 deeded acres but that really doesn't matter. It will never be big enough for a man like him. He has to have more, always more. Greed does that to a man."

"Do you hate him?"

"I try not to hate anyone. I don't like him, but I don't hate the man. Maybe I feel sorry for him. He'll never experience love like we have."

She slowly shook her head. "After all this time," she said, "Sometimes I am still blown away by you Coy."

Coy tried to teach Gunnar how to rope calves that summer. Gunnar tried, but eventually Coy could see he wasn't that interested in calf roping. Gunnar went with him to a local team roping and watched the men catching the heels. On the way home he asked his dad how the man on that end could catch the heels. Coy was surprised because up until then Gunnar had never asked about roping.

The next time Coy was in town, he bought two team roping videos from champion ropers. He put them in the machine and started watching them one night to see if Gunnar would take an interest. The videos were made to help people become better ropers. Gunnar watched the video, sat down and didn't move until it was over. It was late summer and only four weeks until they had to bring the cattle down from the hills. Coy started asking some of the men he knew that had roping horses and knew of other horses for sale. He bought a five-year-old dark bay that wasn't as big as his other ranch horses. Gunnar spotted the horse in the corral that afternoon and asked, "Did you buy another horse?"

"Yeah, I heard about him, looked him over and bought him. He's a five-year-old that has a lot of cow sense in his breeding. He's not as big as our other horses but he is supposed to be a good cow horse. I thought we'd see how he works out. He's about the right size for you or your mother."

Gunnar took up with the young horse and started taking carrots and apples out to him. Gunnar asked his dad if he could ride the new horse when they gathered the cattle out of the BLM ground that year. Coy acted indifferent and said that would be all right. Gunnar rode over to his dad as they were bringing the cattle down.

Grinning, he yelled, "He sure likes to chase cattle." Coy nodded his head.

They had the calves separated from the cows when Gunnar asked, "Do you think he would make a roping horse?"

"He sure has the look and likes to chase

cattle."

While Gunnar pushed the cows out into the larger pen Judith said, "You're getting a little slick aren't you Coy?"

He turned to face her. "Could be," he said with a smile.

They shipped their calves and followed their tradition of paying for a nice meal for the other ranchers that helped haul the cattle up to Trinity, Colorado. All the ranchers did it to thank each other for the help, and have the night out everyone looked forward to.

They picked up Gunnar on the way home. Their son surprised them by bringing home a big stack of gun magazines. He told his folks Phil, owner of the local feed store and close friend to Coy, said he could have them. Later that week, Coy bought six roping steers. He asked Gunnar if he wanted to try out the small horse on the steers in the morning. Gunnar said that would be fun so the two of them watched the roping videos again.

Judith helped them after they finished the morning chores. She opened the head gate when Coy nodded his head. Gunnar missed the first three but caught one hoof on the fourth steer. Then caught both feet on the fifth steer. They kept it up until noon. By then Gunnar could catch one or two feet about half of the time. After they turned out the steers and took care of their horses Coy asked him, "How do you like that horse now?"

"I love him! He puts me where I need to be. I guess he's a natural."

"I guess," said Coy.

Gunnar turned thirteen and Coy noticed that he would do his homework right after supper then read in the gun magazines. He also noticed that Gunnar was shooting his .22 at different ranges and gradually shooting farther. One day in the fall he stopped the ranch flatbed by Gunnar's farthest target and looked at it. It read 110 yards and had a tight group of five shots on it. Every weekend he and Gunnar ran steers through the chute and tried to rope them. Gunnar was getting better.

When spring came, they were able to practice roping more. Early in May, Coy saw a sign at the feed store advertising a local team roping competition. He asked Gunnar if he would like to enter with him. They would split whatever they won.

"Could I buy a new gun?" Gunnar asked.

"It would probably depend on what you wanted to buy."

"A .22 Magnum," Gunnar said quickly. "It has more velocity and will carry its energy way out there."

"That would be okay with me, but we'll have to ask your mother, okay?"

"Sure," said Gunnar.

It was like pulling teeth, but Judith finally agreed. If he won enough, he could buy the rifle. They practiced every chance they could and by the time the roping came up Gunnar was a lot better.

They were walking their horses into the arena when Coy spoke.

"The first time I ever roped at a rodeo, my friend Billy walked up to the arena telling me, 'Just like home, everything here is just like home.' That's what I'm going to tell you now. Don't get nervous or scared, everything here is just like home." Gunnar slowly nodded.

Several of the local cowboys asked Coy who he was roping with. He introduced them to his son. Spider Johnson, the ranch manager at the McDaniels' ranch, came over.

"Coy, if I knew you were going to rope tonight, I would have stayed home and saved my money."

The cowboys close by laughed.

"Spider this is my son, Gunnar," said Coy.

"You were just walking good the last time I saw you Gunnar," said Spider. "Are you heading or heeling tonight?"

"Heeling," said Gunnar.

Spider stuck out his hand and said, "Good luck son." He shook hands with Gunnar then rode over by some other cowboys.

Gunnar watched all kinds of teams rope that night. These weren't professionals and several missed their steer.

"Nobody's real fast tonight," said Coy when their turn came up. "Take your time and catch both feet like at home," he said and smiled.

Gunnar caught both feet with a time of eight point five seconds and they took second place and won a total of $460. Gunnar was quiet on the ride home.

"Anything wrong?" asked Coy.

"I only won $230. I need $279 to buy the

rifle."

"I wouldn't worry about that. I can probably spot you the difference."

Gunnar looked over with a big smile. "Thank you, Dad!" he said. "Now I can make my own sandbags and set up a farther target and really do it right. I want to get better at shooting."

"You're pretty good now."

"I'm going to get better, you wait and see. I've been reading a lot about shooting and guns."

Coy brought home a happy son and a new .22 Magnum Marlin rifle from town the following Saturday. He told Gunnar he wanted to be with him when he set up his target and watch him shoot. That seemed to please Gunnar. The boy set up his target and only came back 25 yards.

"Why only 25 yards?" asked Coy.

"We are just getting it sighted in. After I get the scope the way I want it, we'll start backing up and plotting trajectory."

"Oh," said Coy realizing his son retained a lot from his reading. Coy listened to Gunnar explain what he was doing as he put small pieces of masking tape over each of the holes after he checked his shots. When they moved all the way back to 200 yards Coy asked, "Will that gun really reach that far?"

"Let's find out. If my adjustments are right, it should hit two inches low at this distance so I'll aim at the bull's eye and these rounds should fall just below it." He shot three times then said, "Let's see how they hit."

They drove the farm truck down, got out and looked at the target. Coy slowly turned and looked at his son after seeing the three holes close together and only two inches below the bull's eye. Gunnar didn't seem to be satisfied.

"It should have had a tighter group than that," he said. "I'll have to go back and study my ammunition and see if I can find the problem."

"That's really good for a small caliber."

"But I thought I had everything all mapped out. I'll study some more, and I'll find out what happened."

"That would have killed a coyote."

"Yes, but I like to target shoot. Someday I want to enter shooting contests and there you have to know where that bullet is going to hit every time."

Gunnar came to Coy that night. "I found my answer. We bought a different brand of ammunition than I read about."

"Do you need to change?"

"No, I'll just use these up and then try the other brand and decide which one performs best for my rifle."

Gunnar shot most every day. He and his dad roped steers at least twice a week. Coy had been watching and saw the Trinity Rodeo was coming up across the state line in Colorado. He casually mentioned it at the supper table one evening.

"Think we could win?" Gunnar asked.

"I do, it's just a medium sized rodeo. Most of the professionals won't be there. I think we could do well."

"Let's do it," said Gunnar.

They took Judith and drove up to Trinity and unloaded the horses. Coy paid their entry fees and Judith wished them luck, then went up to sit in the spectator stands. They were warming up their horses in the arena with all the other contestants when a pretty young girl rode up and said, "Hi Gunnar." Gunnar looked over at the girl and her brilliant green barrel racing outfit.

"Hi Jesse," he said. "You going to run barrels?"

"How did you guess?"

Coy laughed. He could tell it embarrassed Gunnar.

"Yeah, I guess that's kind of obvious," he said.

"Are you two going to rope tonight?"

"Yes," said Gunnar.

Coy kept quiet after laughing at the wrong time.

"Well good luck then," she said before riding away.

"Pretty girl," said Coy.

Gunnar glared at him.

"Fast," said Coy just before they walked their horses into the roping boxes. Coy nodded his head to the men working chute and flew out of the header's box. He caught the steer and turned him in a slow arc. He saw Gunnar's rope come tight and saw the steer's two feet caught in the loop.

"Seven and six tenths seconds!" the

announcer yelled in the microphone. "We have a new leader!" the man added.

Coy liked the way Gunnar was modest to all the compliments from the other cowboys. They had to wait to get their money and Coy could tell Gunnar had something on his mind.

In a low voice Gunnar said, "I'm just going to ride my horse over there for a minute."

Coy didn't know why he would do that until he saw the pickup drive into the arena with the barrels for the barrel racing event. He smiled remembering that pretty girl in the green outfit. He tied his horse on the trailer and walked over to where he could watch the girls running the barrels. He knew which one his son would be rooting for.

The first four ran well with number three being the fastest. When the fifth horse came racing in, he recognized the flashy green outfit. She did fine on her first turn, then knocked down the barrel on the second turn and her horse shied wide of the barrel. She was fighting to get control of him. She finally did and ran at half speed for the last barrel. When she rounded the last one, she spurred her horse and flew across the finish line and far out into the parking area. Coy stood high on the fence and saw his son riding her way.

He thought she needed help with her horse, so he rode his horse over there. What he found was her standing on the ground being hugged by his son while she cried hard. He could see Gunnar patting her on the back, so Coy turned his horse around and rode back to the trailer.

Judith came up and asked where Gunnar was.

"He was over there hugging that girl in the green barrel racing outfit, the last time I saw him."

"He's not even fourteen."

"He almost is, and I didn't see any kissing, he's okay."

Judith walked back and forth for a while looking in that direction. She stopped and said, "I think we better go find him now." Coy smiled and looked down.

"I don't think that's necessary, here they come now," he said. Judith looked to see the two kids riding their way. The girl stopped before she got close and held out her hand. Gunnar grabbed it and Coy saw him say, "That's okay." Then, Gunnar walked his horse up to his parents. Coy started loading his horse and saddle. He wanted to be doing something, anything when the questions started.

"Who was that?" asked Judith.

"Just a girl from school."

"Are you two seeing each other?"

Gunnar looked at her.

"Are you dating her?"

"No Mom, she's just a girl from school that really blew it tonight in front of a big crowd of people. She was crying her eyes out and I tried to help."

"I guess that covers that, let's unsaddle your horse, load him up, get our money and head home," said Coy.

Judith glared at him. Gunnar laughed lightly at his dad. They were driving out of the rodeo grounds when Judith finally spoke.

"You are way too young to start dating."

"I agree, especially since I don't have a driver's license," said Gunnar.

That tickled Coy but he kept from laughing.

"I just want you to have good control of your life, that's all."

"I know Mom, I know. You don't have anything to worry about."

"All right then," said Judith finally satisfied. "And you Coy," she said, "You stop that smiling over there."

Coy burst out laughing, and Gunnar did too. Judith just shook her head and said, "You two."

Coy elbowed his son just a little on his right side. Judith went in the house when they got home, and the guys unloaded the horses and saddles at the barn.

"I think it would be better if you told me how everything happened with that girl tonight, because I think your mother is going to ask me."

"Nothing happened."

"I know that, just tell me how you came to be hugging her."

"I didn't really hug her, she hugged me."

"I thought it would be something like that."

"I walked up just as she slid off her horse crying, then she was crying on my shirt. I didn't know what to do so I patted her on the back and told her it would be okay."

Coy was smiling when he said, "For that you get grilled by your mother."

"Exactly."

"Is Jesse's last name McDaniels?"

"Yes, it is, how come?"

"I just wondered who she was. Don't give it a second thought. Your mother will have to talk to me about it and I'll casually let it out what you told me. But I do have to say one thing. Jesse sure is a cute little thing."

Gunnar looked at his dad and shook his head.

CHAPTER 2

A Rifle Good Enough

The rest of the summer Gunnar concentrated on his shooting and they only roped about once a week. Then school was getting ready to start and Gunnar took more of an interest in the school clothes his mother bought.

Coy noticed that he started looking better in the mornings before school. Evidently that hug had woke him up a little he thought to himself. Before the end of October, Gunnar was in the feed store with his dad, when he had Coy follow him over to the bulletin board. There was a flyer for a competitive target shooting contest at Santa Fe. The winner could win $250.

"I think we should talk to Phil," said Gunnar. "He used to compete in contests like these." They stopped by Phil's house on the way home. He filled them in on all the main details of a target shoot.

"If Gunnar is serious about competing, he can't start shooting too early," he told Coy.

"Would you consider going with us?" Coy asked.

"I would love to, and I'll bring some things I think you'll need," he said. "One thing you need to know, there aren't age groupings at these things. He'll be shooting against adults, but the sooner he starts, the better his chances are of getting really good."

In Santa Fe, Coy could see that Gunnar didn't have a good enough rifle as they walked around the shooting range. These shooters had rifles with thick barrels and special stocks. They found the shooting tables they were to shoot from and drove the truck close.

Phil said, "Let's take my cases."

They hauled the large wooden cases over to the shooting tables. Phil opened one of his cases and took out a bench rest.

He smiled at Gunnar and said, "It's an older one but it still works."

He set it on the table and showed Gunnar how to use it. Then he opened his other case. Coy was taken back and Gunnar's mouth hung open.

"How about we let Gunnar use my rifle today?" Phil asked

Inside the case was a rifle with a thick barrel

and a heavy wooden stock like the other men had. Phil smiled when he said, "It's a target rifle with a bull barrel chambered to .223 caliber because the ammo is relatively cheap. It weighs 14 pounds so the recoil should only be slightly more than your .22 Magnum."

Gunnar stared at the gun.

"We had better get it out and let him shoot so the folks behind us get a chance to shoot," said Phil. After they got him set up and they got the go ahead to fire, Phil came over and stood by Coy.

"Watch his form," he said. "The gun should move, and he shouldn't blink."

The rifle went off and Phil looked at Coy and slowly nodded his head. He leaned close and said, "He is going to get good. He has perfect form."

The range master finally gave the order to stop shooting and retrieve targets. Gunnar brought his back and Phil told him to turn it in for measurement.

When he was gone Phil told Coy, "I'm going to give my rifle to Gunnar."

"I really wish you wouldn't do that," said Coy concerned. "He needs to earn it. Either save his money or work for you, but he needs to work for it."

"I would love for him to have it," said Phil. "Neither one of our two sons like to shoot, and Gunnar can be something. He's always asking me questions about calibers and ranges and recoil. You saw him shoot. He has that total concentration that good shooters have."

Gunnar came back with a big smile. "They asked how old I was," he said showing them the target with the measurement written on it.

"Just a little over half an inch at 200 yards," said Phil. "Not bad for your first time."

"What do we do now?" asked Coy.

"Sit around and twiddle our thumbs," said Phil. "I suggest we go get something to eat and come back. That way maybe we won't have to wait so long."

"Should we clean your rifle first?" asked Gunnar.

"Oh, I think it will keep until we get home," said Phil.

They had a great meal at an Italian restaurant and were back in little over an hour. Phil took Gunnar over to the table where the officials were measuring the remaining targets.

"What is ranked third right now at 200 yards?" he asked

"Point four eight five inches right now," the man said. Phil thanked him and walked back over to Coy.

"We're out of the running by less than a quarter of an inch. Gunnar got nosed out."

"Out of how many shooters?" asked Coy.

"Let's see," said Phil. He was back in a few minutes and said "They just checked out target number 118 and have a few more to go. Do you want to stay and hear the awards or leave?"

"I'm ready to go," said Gunnar. "I had a ball. I got to shoot against grown men and did alright."

In the pickup Gunnar said, "Now that was

fun."

Then he asked Phil about his target rifle. Coy drove and listened. At his house Phil told them that he had had a great time and would go again any time they wanted to.

That night in bed after the lights were out, Judith asked, "How good is he?"

"He took fourth place out of about 120 grown men with a gun that he never fired before. Phil said he has what it takes to get really good."

"But is shooting a gun something we want him to get really good at?"

"I don't think we have a choice. He picked it, we didn't. If you were to see him around Phil asking questions and thinking about the answers you would see that it's his passion. Roping is okay but nothing compared to shooting. Besides that, if we tried to make him stop, he would just want to do it more."

"Yeah I can see that."

Phil brought a newspaper clipping out to the ranch Monday afternoon. It talked about the target shooting competition and gave Gunnar's name. 'Also, a contestant named Gunnar Danewood received honorable mention being only thirteen years old and taking fourth place.' He was the youngest contestant at the event it said.

"Wow," said Judith.

"That's really something," said Coy. Gunnar just smiled.

"I've been thinking," said Phil. "I don't shoot my rifle anymore and Gunnar did really well with it. I was wondering if next spring and summer I could hire him to help me work at my house and he could work out the cost of the rifle."

Coy looked over at Judith. She was watching her son. Gunnar was so excited he could hardly sit still.

"Please Mom, please, if I could shoot that gun more, I could win that contest down at Santa Fe."

When she looked over to Coy, he knew she was going to agree to it.

"How would we do it?" Coy asked.

"I'll keep a running total of the hours he works, and we'll have to set a price on the rifle. He can see my figures any time he wants to and see where he's at," said Phil.

The adults talked and came up with a plan of Gunnar driving the older ranch pickup almost to the city limits, then taking his bicycle out of the bed and riding it up to Phil's house. They set the value of the rifle at $800. Coy asked Gunnar if he was going to stick with it and follow through till all the money was worked off or paid for.

"Absolutely," said Gunnar with an expression that showed he meant it. Before he left, Phil told them that if Coy gave him a call, he would bring the rifle out and let Gunnar shoot it any time he wanted to on the ranch.

Gunnar asked to be left at Phil's house when his parents shipped their calves that fall. When they picked him up to go home, he told them about reloading some shells for the target rifle.

Coy caught Judith's eye and winked at her. Gunnar talked all the way out to the ranch about reloading.

Winter came and so did all the long heavy workdays. Coy would leave early and come back in for a late breakfast, then go out again and stay until mid-afternoon. Then he would come back in, eat a light lunch before going out again. Judith would go out with him most of the time in the late afternoons to help and that's the way the winter passed.

Gunnar started driving out to the edge of town in mid-April. His first job for Phil was raking and burning leaves. Then it was helping his wife Jean in her flowerbeds. Just before school was out, he and Phil started painting the outside of the house. They would usually go out to Phil's shop and work on ammunition right after lunch to let their food settle. After a while they would go back to work.

Haying season started in late July and Coy asked Gunnar how much was left on the rifle. Gunnar said he had earned over $600 so far. Coy told him he needed him home until they were finished putting up the hay. Gunnar told his dad that he would tell Phil the next afternoon. Coy suggested they practice roping in the cool mornings before the dew came off the fields.

"It will keep us tuned up and maybe we could win a little money. Then you could pay out the balance of the rifle," he said.

Gunnar jumped on that. They roped almost every morning and put up hay in the afternoons. The Raton town rodeo was coming up before school started and Coy asked Gunnar about it. In his usual quiet manner Gunnar said, "I think we should enter it and win, Dad." Coy laughed.

Judith packed some sandwiches and they drove the pickup and horse trailer to the rodeo grounds. The men warmed up their horses in the dusty arena. Coy caught Gunnar looking around.

"Think she'll show?" he asked.

Gunnar looked over at him with a puzzled expression.

"You know that girl from school that wears that flashy green barrel outfit," said Coy with a smile. Gunnar shook his head slowly and looked away. Coy thought with the rodeo in Raton she would show up.

After about thirty minutes some of the cowboys were starting to leave the arena when Coy saw one horse moving much faster than the others. She was moving in and out and around the other horses.

"Hi Gunnar!" she yelled as she rode her horse past them.

"Hi," he said loud enough for her to hear as she rode away. Neither father nor son spoke, then Gunnar said, "See Dad, that girl in the flashy green outfit didn't show. She's wearing a flashy red outfit."

Coy laughed and said, "Just a girl from school."

Gunnar looked over at his laughing father who raised his eyebrows at him.

"I don't know why I put up with you," said Gunnar as they walked out of the arena.

Judith was waiting at the trailer after they had caught their steer. She told them how great they did but Coy was listening to the other ropers' times.

Gunnar told his mother, "He won't listen until the last team makes their run."

All three heard the announcer say the last team broke the barrier and that put them out of the competition.

"We won!" said Coy.

"Great!" said Gunnar, "Now maybe I can pay off my rifle. I'm going to go say hi to some kids from school," Gunnar said reining his horse around. Judith looked over at Coy.

"Let him go. We almost live in isolation. He needs to socialize with other kids."

She turned and looked at her son on his horse walking away. "Is she here?" she asked.

"I didn't see any flashy green outfit tonight," Coy said. She tilted her head forward and down like she always did when she was serious.

"Yes, she's here."

"He's going over there to see her, isn't he?"

"More than likely, I guess," said Coy taking the saddle off his horse.

"Let's go over there and watch."

"Judith we can't do that," he said as he stopped putting stuff in the trailer. He turned to face her.

"He's young but he has a life too and we need to respect that."

"I don't want him dating yet." she said.

"I don't think he is. I think he is just starting to look at girls a little."

"Kids are growing up a lot faster these days."

"I know and I know my son. Right now, he wants to be around girls but doesn't know what to say or how to act."

Judith stared at him.

"I'll tell you what, how about we load up everything and drive over there and ask him if he's ready to go, how's that?"

Judith liked that.

Coy loaded up everything and together they slowly drove over in the direction they had seen Gunnar go. They found him sitting on his horse talking to several other kids all sitting on horses. Coy noticed the girl in the red barrel outfit was next to Gunnar. Coy stopped the truck and said, "I'll just go get him."

He opened the swing gate of the trailer and when Gunnar didn't come over, he walked over to the kids. "Ready to go?" he asked just before the other truck and trailer drove up. Darlene McDaniels got out and started towards the kids.

Coy saw Darlene then looked over and saw the girl reach out her hand to Gunnar who took it and they said goodbye. He was walking his horse towards Coy when Darlene yelled out, "Hey you!"

Gunnar stopped his horse and turned to look at her. Coy reached up and grabbed the horse's reins.

"Stay away from my daughter!" Darlene yelled at Gunnar.

Coy then saw two things happen. Darlene's daughter dropped her head in embarrassment. Gunnar leaned back in the saddle in amazement that this woman would yell at him like that. Then Coy heard his pickup door open.

"You don't have to worry about our son, why don't you keep your daughter away from him!" Judith yelled.

"Time to leave son," said Coy pulling on the horse's reins. Gunnar kept looking at the woman who had yelled at him.

"I mean what I'm saying!" yelled Darlene.

"Go ahead and climb down," said Coy.

"So do we!" yelled Judith.

Gunnar was on the ground looking back at Jesse's mother. Coy went ahead and loaded Gunnar's horse with the saddle on and closed the gate.

"Time to go," he said gently leading him by the elbow. Gunnar was shaking his head as he climbed up in the cab. Coy stepped in front of his wife blocking her view. "Don't embarrass him any more tonight. Let's just leave, okay?"

She glared past him at the girl's mother but when he gently touched her elbow, she nodded and got in the truck. Coy thought he could hear Darlene yelling something as they drove away.

"What's her problem?" asked Gunnar.

Judith turned her head and gave Coy a look. Coy squirmed a little in his seat before he started.

"She and I used to date in high school. I said I would like to be married to her and she took that as a proposal. I ran into her at the grocery store and told her I didn't want to get married and she's hated my guts ever since."

It was quiet for a few miles down the road until Gunnar said, "You did kind of leave her at the altar."

"There's a little more to it than that."

"No wonder she hates you."

Coy nodded his head yes.

"Have you ever apologized?" Gunnar asked.

"After you saw her tonight, you might understand how I never had the opportunity."

"Mom, did you know this?"

"I've known all along."

Gunnar looked out his window and slowly began to smile.

"Mom, weren't you afraid he would leave you at the altar too?"

"Hey now!" yelled Coy.

Gunnar started laughing and so did Judith. Coy shook his head and grinned. "That was a low shot son, real low." From then on everyone was happy all the way home.

Coy went into town the next day and picked up the $900 that they won at the rodeo. He came back and gave Gunnar his money at lunch. Gunnar said he wanted to keep on working at Phil's house and keep his winnings for something later. Coy suggested that he start a bank account. Judith nodded her head and said, "It's never too early for a young man to start managing his money."

Gunnar stopped working at Phil's house after lunch and rode his bike over to the bank and tried to open a savings account. He found out that an adult had to sign with him to get an account. He was outside getting on his bike when he heard the boy's voice.

"There he is," the voice said loudly. "There's the kid that got his name in the paper for being lucky down at Santa Fe." Gunnar looked over at the front of the hardware store next door and there was Nicholas Everett standing there with two younger boys. Big Nick as the local boys called him, was the local loudmouth at school among the boys that were Gunnar's age.

"I guess he's just trying to live up to his name," Nick yelled out. "Yep, Danewood is a Gunnar all right." The other boys laughed at Nick's words.

Gunnar was the tallest kid in his class except for Nick who had been held back in the third grade. Everyone knew he was touchy about that. The story was he had beat up several boys who had made a comment about it.

"That's me," Gunnar yelled, then rode his bicycle back over to Phil's house.

CHAPTER 3

Big Nick

School started and Gunnar paid Phil the remaining sixty dollars he owed from his rodeo money. Phil told him any time he wanted to come over and reload his ammunition, it was fine with him. Coy noticed that Gunnar was even more interested in buying his school clothes. His son was starting to grow up. Gunnar caught the bus at the end of their driveway like always. The Danewoods sold their calves and got ready for winter.

Gunnar shot every chance the weather would allow. He talked to Phil and found that his words were true about shooting often but not firing a lot of rounds. That helped to keep his costs down. He still liked helping his dad feed the cattle on the weekends. He was in middle school and there were three school dances a year, but he never went. He was more interested in guns and shooting. He also started growing and eating a lot more. He was barely fourteen and only two inches shorter than Coy.

Coy, Phil and Gunnar went down to Santa Fe for the target shoot. Coy entered him again and saw that his son was more relaxed. Gunnar took third place and won a small trophy. On the way home he told his dad, "I told you I'd get better."

Spring came and Coy noticed that Gunnar was distant and moody. Grass was starting to show but they were still feeding a lot of hay. One weekend they unrolled the last bale for the morning and were ready to drive home when Coy spoke.

"When I was your age, sometimes at a time like this when it was just me and my dad, I would talk to him about something that bothered me."

Gunnar sat there but Coy could tell it would come out if he gave him time.

"There's this big kid at school," he finally said. "He's kind of a bully. He's always got something to say about me. He won't stop and I think he'll want to fight."

"And?" asked Coy.

Gunnar had to look down to say it, but he finally got it out. "And I'm afraid of him."

"Is that all? I thought it was something big."

Gunnar looked up really surprised.

"I can help you with that. What's this kid's name?"

"Nick Everett"

"Bud Everett's boy?"

"Yes."

"His dad was a bully when we were in high school. I guess it just runs in the family. Listen, I've never said anything, but my dad was a state boxing champion. He taught me how to fight and I can teach you. You ever see this kid fight?"

"No," Gunnar said softly.

"How is he built?"

"He's just big, that's all I know."

"If he's big and hasn't trained he'll be slow. I'll teach you all you need to know. You ever notice all that stuff in the corner of the tack room?"

"Yes."

"We'll get it out and I'll teach you how to fight. Don't let him prod you into a fight until you're ready. Then you pick the time and place and clean his clock."

"He's really big Dad."

"Big doesn't count, speed counts. It's like chopping down a tree. That's what my dad used to say. Now try not to let it bother you anymore. His time will come, trust me on this."

They rode in silence for a while until Gunnar asked, "So your dad was a boxing champion?"

"Not just a boxing champion, a state boxing champion. I used to watch him on the speed bag and wonder if I could ever do that. It takes patience and practice and determination. Then comes a person's coordination and balance. I was never as good as him, but I learned quite a lot."

"Did you ever fight anyone?"

"Yep, Nick's dad in fact. I gave him a lesson he's never forgotten. He was bigger than me and he knew it would be easy. Never, never take your opponent for granted, my dad used to say."

By mid-afternoon they had everything set up in the far two stalls at the back of the barn.

"This is going to take time, probably months. You learn to walk before you learn to run so we'll go over the basics, then will come the fun stuff. What you learn here will never leave you. Another thing we need to come up with is something to tell your mother. How about you are thinking about trying to box?"

"Yeah, that's good."

"You're also going to have to run."

"How far?"

"Three miles five times a week. It will be hard at first, but eventually you'll look forward to it. I always ran in the early mornings. It was my time to do my thing if that makes any sense."

"I think I understand that."

"We should get you a small set of weights. We will use them to build strength in your arms for power on the delivery. This is going to be fun," said Coy smiling.

They started the next morning. Coy drove down to feed on the far west end and Gunnar ran all the way down then climbed into the truck just before his dad finished unrolling the last bale of hay. They came back and ate breakfast then sat around for over half an hour. Coy stood up and said, "I'm going down to the barn want to come?"

"You bet," said Gunnar. Coy pushed the body bag to get it swinging and showed him how to hit it and how to throw combinations of punches one after the other. Then he talked about his feet and balance. When he was tired, Coy had him try the speed bag. Gunnar couldn't find the rhythm.

"If you stick with it, by the end of summer you'll be able to make this thing sing," he said before hitting the speed bag and making it move so fast Gunnar couldn't believe it.

"Now for the last lesson of the day. Hold up your hands and don't let me touch your face." Coy faked his right and quickly touched Gunnar's face with his left. "Don't let me touch you," he said again. Coy threw a right, left, then threw out an open left. Gunnar knocked it away.

"Excellent, we want to do this when you are tired until it becomes completely instinctive. When something is headed your way, you block it and knock it away. Tomorrow I want you to move as you hit the bag. A moving target is always harder to hit than a stationary one."

Coy let Gunnar sleep in a little on Monday morning. As they worked in the barn that afternoon, he told him he would start waking him in the mornings. Gunnar ran in the morning and worked out in the barn after school. Coy waited a full month before he bought a set of dumbbells for Gunnar to use. He also bought small weights to put on Gunnar's wrists. "You're doing really good," he told his son. "These on your wrist will make your fists fast as lightning."

Judith came out and saw what they were doing. She told them she didn't like what was going on but accepted it. Summer came and Gunnar ran farther. Coy had him lifting the dumbbells using the same movements as punches at the end of the workout. Now Coy couldn't touch Gunnar's face no matter how hard he tried.

"It's time to spar a little," Coy told him before they started baling hay in late July. The first evening they sparred, Gunnar caught Coy with a short right and gave him a black eye. Coy told him the reason he had hit him was because now Gunnar was so fast that he couldn't get his hands over in time. "You need to learn more, but you've already come a long way," he said.

Gunnar ran early then helped his dad in the hay fields. He also started eating a sandwich before bedtime after eating a big evening meal. His dad could see him getting taller and stronger.

They finished putting up hay for the year and Coy surprised Gunnar by buying him a nice older pickup truck for him to drive when he turned fifteen and got a farm permit.

One week before school started, Coy told Gunnar to start unloading on the body bag. "You're fast," he said, "now it's time to try and drive your fist all the way through the bag. Concentrate and push off the floor, let all the power come up through your lower back, out your arm and try to destroy the bag."

Coy could see it was a little awkward at first but slowly it all came together. The last evening before school, Coy told him, "Remember this, it is between him and you, not the whole school. Pick a time when there are only a few kids around. You don't want a reputation as a fighter because then you'll have to fight all the time. We will keep training and you will get some better, but you're ready now. Just remember speed and power.

"Above all don't let him stomp you when or if you go down. Roll, crawl, do anything but get back up. All your training goes down the drain if you are on the ground." Gunnar was nodding his head that he understood. "Now comes the most important lesson. You have the skill, never be afraid again. Only fight if you need to, not because you want to. Boxing in the ring is different. If done correctly it is a sport."

Coy watched Gunnar when he came in from school and saw a different boy. He was much more self-assured and not as serious. He still didn't talk much but joked around more than he ever had. The young man was coming into his own. Coy watched for signs of a fight but saw none. Gunnar ran and worked out in the barn after school. He only missed Wednesday's when he would shoot his target rifle. Then on Saturday afternoons he would shoot again.

The three men went down to Santa Fe for

the target shoot that fall, and Gunnar took third place again out of over 250 shooters. On the way home Phil told him, "You have really improved. You are now in the top one half of one per cent of all the men that competed today. I don't know anyone, man or boy that can say that."

Gunnar thanked him and smiled. Then he looked out his window and kept smiling.

Gunnar made the papers again. It was on the front page of the sports page in the Santa Fe newspaper. Coy bought three copies for Judith to cut out the article about Gunnar. It seemed everyone in town and at school had heard about it. Nick Everett made a point of speaking loud in the school cafeteria.

"Yep," he said, "Shooter Danewood, the great shot from Raton. He is so great he can't do better than third place."

All the kids that were close enough to hear saw Gunnar smile and say, "Seems that way doesn't it." He winked at one girl standing at the edge of the group.

Gunnar was on his way into town Saturday afternoon a week later, when he heard shooting coming from the city dump. He pulled in and saw Nick's Everett's old brown pickup parked and several kids standing around. He parked over to one side and walked over.

"Well if it's not Shooter Danewood, the great shot from Raton," said Nick, trying to once again make fun of Gunnar.

"That would be me," Gunnar said smiling. "What's up, I heard some shooting?"

"I was just trying to get Billy to put a pop bottle on his head and let me shoot it off," said Nick.

Gunnar's expression changed from a smile to a look of complete seriousness. "You aren't really going to let him do that are you Billy?"

"Well I was kind of thinking I might," said the kid two years younger than the rest of the group.

"That's not something to mess around with. IIis forearm could slip, or his shoe could slide, and he could shoot you right in the head."

"Shooters just scared that's all, Billy walk out there and put the bottle on your head," said Nick.

"I don't know, what Gunnar said makes a lot of sense."

"Here," said Jesse McDaniels, "I'll put it on my head," she said grabbing the bottle. Gunnar took three quick steps and grabbed the bottle away from her.

"No you won't, don't be stupid."

"Hey Danewood, if she wants to do it, let her," said Nick bristling up.

Gunnar leaned down and said quietly, "Go stand by my truck, when this is over, I'll give you a ride home." Then he looked up at Nick Everett. "You know Nick you've been prodding me for over a year now. If I didn't know better, I would think you wanted to fight."

"Ha," yelled Nick, "think you can fight me?"

"I don't want to, but I'll fight if that's what you want."

"This is going to be fun," said Nick putting

his rifle in the front seat of his truck.

"Better unload that rifle first, we don't want anybody shot."

"I always keep my guns loaded," said Nick with a laugh.

"I see," said Gunnar.

They faced each other and Gunnar slowly moved to his left, "Come on and get what it is that you want."

Nick kind of jumped forward and swung with his right hand. Gunnar went under it and tried for Nick's solar plexus but missed and hooked him hard on his lower right rib cage. Nick spun around and Gunnar jabbed him twice right on the nose.

Nick was mad and charged forward and this time Gunnar went to his right. He set his feet and when Nick turned ,Gunnar nailed him on his jaw a little high, missing his chin. The punch knocked Nick back, so Gunnar came forward with two left jabs then a right. He was knocking the big kid back punch by punch. Nick now had his hands up trying to protect his face.

Gunnar dropped his hands and said, "What's the matter, I thought you wanted to fight?"

Nick came forward again but now he was being careful. Gunnar moved side to side on his feet and jabbed Nick in the face before he could cover it up. Then Gunnar jumped forward and Nick tried to go backwards but bumped into his own pickup. He turned to see what it was, and Gunnar drove his left fist into and upward in Nick's solar plexus knocking all the air out of the big kid. Gunnar pulled his right hand back and nailed Nick right behind his left ear, and the bully fell on his face in the dirt.

"Now," said Gunnar, "We are going to unload that rifle before somebody accidentally shoots someone." He took the rifle out of the truck and emptied all the shells out on the ground.

"Let's let Nick pick up his own shells today," he said to the rest of the kids standing there. Then he went over and opened his passenger door for Jesse and said, "Get in the truck."

He drove for a few minutes before starting in on her.

"That was stupid! What in the world were you thinking? Agreeing to let some clown shoot a pop bottle off your head. Tell me something!" he yelled. "Have you ever seen an animal shot in the head, then fall down and start kicking and thrashing around?"

"No," she said quietly.

"Well today that could have been you. That was stupid, just plain stupid," he yelled.

She clouded up and burst out crying. He clamped his jaw and looked out his window. She didn't stop crying and they were halfway to her house.

"Okay, I guess I was a little hard on you, but you can't be doing that kind of stuff."

She slowly began to let up and when she felt she could talk she said, "You are just mean."

"Yeah, I guess so, mean enough to keep you from getting shot in the head today."

She saw him smile and wiped her tears away

on her shirt sleeve.

He gave her his clean handkerchief and said, "You better get dried up a little before we get you home. The way your mother feels about me, if she sees you crying, she might shoot me."

That made the young girl laugh lightly. She gave him a weak smile. He stopped just inside the entrance to the McDaniel ranch.

"What should we do, stop here or drive all the way up to the house?"

"My mom's shopping down at Santa Fe, that's how I was able to get away today. You can drive up to the house."

"Okay," said Gunnar putting his truck in gear. "I want to give you the same advice my dad gave me last year. He said, 'It's okay to be a little dumb, but don't be stupid.' Okay?" he asked as he stopped in front of the huge house.

"Okay," she said quietly, "I was only trying to get you to notice me."

He leaned his head over and put his chin on his right arm just below his shoulder. "Oh, I've noticed you Jesse. I would have to be blind not to notice a girl as pretty as you."

That did the trick, she was back to her spunky self. She reached up and squeezed his arm. "Thanks for the ride," she said smiling.

"It was my pleasure," he said not moving his chin off his arm. She got out and yelled bye just as he drove away.

Coy saw Gunnar's hands but Judith didn't notice them until supper that night.

"What happened to your hands?" she asked. Gunnar looked at his dad.

"There's no need to look at your father, I'm over here," she said. "Now tell me what happened to your hands."

"I bruised them on a big kid's face," he said and laughed.

Coy laughed until Judith shot him a look.

Then she leaned back in her chair. "So that's what all this has been about," she said slowly nodding her head. "And you two decided to keep me in the dark all this time."

"Yes ma'am," said Gunnar.

She slowly turned and faced Coy.

"Is there anything you would like to say to me Coy Danewood?"

"There are feelings a girl or woman will never understand. A man needs to believe in himself. If he has enough faith in his abilities, failure doesn't defeat him. It is only a setback. Gunnar used boxing to find himself and overcome his fears."

"And just who was this fear?" she asked.

"Nick Everett," said father and son at the same time.

"And what's so special about this Everett boy?"

"He's big, real big," said Gunnar.

"And he's a bully," said Coy, "Or he used to be a bully anyway. Your son cleaned his clock."

"And you think it was right keeping it from me all this time?"

"Yes, we did, and still do think it was the right thing to do. You would have tried to protect him and told him not to fight that kid."

Judith lightened up after that. The three had

a quiet evening and just before bedtime Judith told them, "I've thought all evening about this. I see your motives and I see it was a man thing, but no more secrets."

"Okay Mom," said Gunnar.

"No more secrets," said Coy.

"Come here," Judith said to her son. She turned his face side to side. "Did he even hit you?"

"No ma'am"

"And you're not hurt?"

"Only my fists," he said.

CHAPTER 4

The Trip to Trinity

Things went back to normal. It was school for Gunnar and taking care of the cattle for his parents. The kids at school heard about the fight and if anything, Gunnar was more popular. It seemed to him that girls always had some dumb question to ask.

Christmas time was coming. Coy and Judith were in the town cafe and heard that there was going to be a calf roping jackpot on the nineteenth of December in an indoor arena up in Trinity. Since it was on a weekday and he hadn't done anything for fun in a while, he told his friends at the cafe he would go. He could see Adam McDaniels sitting in a corner booth by himself with a scowl on his face.

On the nineteenth, Judith stayed home and took care of Gunnar who had an upset stomach. He told her to go with Coy, but she smiled at him, so he gave up and laid back down. It was not quite dark when the State Police car pulled up in the front yard. The trooper was very serious when he asked, "Are you Mrs. Judith Danewood?"

"Yes," she said.

"Mrs. Danewood, there has been an accident and your husband has been badly injured," the trooper said. It hit her like a spear in her chest. "Your husband has been transported to the Trinity Hospital and I believe is now being flown to a trauma center in Colorado Springs. We arranged for me to drive you there in my patrol car if you wish." Judith was having a hard time breathing. The trooper said, "Maybe you should sit down for a moment." He helped her into the house and closed the front door.

"Gunnar," she said softly.

"What ma'am?" the trooper asked

"Call my son, his name is Gunnar."

"Gunnar!" the trooper called out. Gunnar came running down the hall in his underwear hearing the strange voice in the house.

"Tell him," she said still trying to breathe normally. The state trooper quickly told Gunnar.

"Go put some clothes on," she told her son. Gunnar came back fully dressed. Judith started to leave without a coat.

"You'll need a coat ma'am," said the trooper. Then he grabbed Gunnar by the arm. "She's had quite a shock, you are going to have to look out for her."

Gunnar looked the man in the eyes and quickly nodded.

The state trooper didn't run his siren but used his lights and sped all the way to Colorado Springs. He told them that another vehicle hit Coy's truck on the driver side door and knocked Coy's truck clear off the highway. The emergency responders used the Jaws of life to get him out. Unfortunately, the horse had to be shot on site.

"The other vehicle didn't stop," he said and looked over at Judith solemnly. "It's been written up as a hit and run."

The trooper used his radio and found the name and address of the hospital. He helped get them up to a waiting room for families of surgery patients. They thanked him for his help, and he left. While they were sitting there, Gunnar asked if she had contacted anyone. She just slowly shook her head.

She dug around in her purse and gave money to Gunnar. He went down to the payphone in the lobby and called Phil, early that morning. Gunnar told him what had happened and asked Phil to call the neighbors and have them look after the cattle for a few days. He ended the call by saying, "We will call when we know something."

Gunnar was walking back in when he saw his mom talking to a doctor. She was crying. Gunnar walked up and put one arm around his mother.

"Your father is holding his own," he said. "He took one horrific hit. His left arm is broken, his left leg is broken in two places and he has broken ribs on that side. Currently it is his brain we are worried about. His skull was cracked. We drilled three small holes in it to relieve the pressure on his brain from swelling. We are administering anti-swelling drugs through an IV. Now for the good news," he said. "Your father is in unbelievable good shape, like an athlete. We put him into an induced coma until the danger is passed from the swelling in his skull. I see all kinds of people here, but I think your dad is one who has no quit in him. I really believe he is going to pull through this."

Gunnar was looking at the man but could feel his tears rolling down his face. "How long until we know for sure?" he asked.

"Usually seven to nine days, but with your father, I believe it will be less," he said.

"Thank you," Gunnar said shaking the man's hand and wiping away his tears. He helped his shaking mother over to a chair and they sat down. The doctors allowed them to go into the intensive care room one at a time.

Gunnar stood and said, "Let me go first." Judith slowly nodded her head.

Gunnar thought he was ready, but he wasn't. Coy's head was swollen so bad it was hard to tell who he was.

"He's breathing on his own," a nurse said walking into the room. "That is really something after what he has been through."

Gunnar nodded his head and said, "I'm worried about my mother when she sees him."

"Women are a lot stronger than you men think we are, she'll be fine," the nurse said.

"Just watch out for her, okay?"

"Sure, I will," the nurse said.

He came out and sat by his mother. "He's doing as good as he can," he said. "He's breathing on his own and his heart is strong. He looks rough, Mom. He is all swollen up and you can hardly recognize him, so be ready for a shock, okay?"

She nodded her head, crying softly.

"I think maybe you should say the words before you go in there," said Gunnar. She reached up and put her hand on his face.

She wiped her tears away, took in a big breath, let it out and said, "Okay I'm ready."

"Okay Mom," said Gunnar walking beside her to the door.

She thought she was ready but when she saw him, she went weak in her knees and started to wilt. The nurse stepped forward and helped her into a chair.

"I know he looks rough but he's doing much better than he looks. He is breathing on his own and his heart is strong. You have quite a man there Mrs. Danewood."

"He is the light of my life," Judith got out looking up at her.

"There is no science to back it up, but when two people are close, I think it helps for their loved one to talk to them."

"What should I say?"

"Tell him you love him and everything you are going to do when he gets out of here."

Judith rocked back and forth in her chair for almost a minute and a half and then started talking to Coy.

"Coy, you would be so proud of Gunnar if you saw how he has been taking care of me. He has stepped up and is handling things. When we get you out of here, I think we should go somewhere. Maybe we could go down to Santa Fe. Remember when we bought our rings down there. That might be fun. We can go anywhere you like. First you have to get better so we can take you home."

The nurse left the room.

"We are alone now, and I want to tell you how much I love you. My life, my and Gunnar's lives, were headed down the drain until you took us in. You are the light of my life. I can't even imagine life without you in it. Get better Coy, please get better. I need you so bad." Then she began to cry and thought it best to leave the room.

The hospital had a few rooms where family members could sleep if they weren't local. Judith and Gunnar took turns sitting with Coy, then sleeping in the room.

It happened on the fourth night. Judith fell asleep sitting in a chair in Coy's room when something woke her. It was a fragrance, a sweet light woman's fragrance. She stood and looked around the room. There was no one there. Then she stepped to the door and looked out. Walking away was a woman whose fragrance was now in the hall. Judith knew she was supposed to recognize something about that woman. Then it hit her, the boots, those high dollar, smooth-leather, cowboy boots. The woman walked into the elevator, turned, pushed a button and held her handkerchief up to her mouth as she cried. Darlene McDaniels slowly raised her head and saw Judith watching her. She shook out her hair in defiance and stared at Judith until the doors closed.

"Well, well," said Judith before going back into Coy's room.

They cut the medicine and let Coy come out of his coma on the sixth day. It took another eight hours for him to open his eyes.

"Hello, my love," were the first words he heard Judith say. He tried to speak but couldn't. His left arm was secured, so he slowly moved his right arm. She went over to it and held his hand and kissed it.

"I'm glad you're back," she said. He began to look all around at everything. "You have been in a serious accident." she said. She could see the words slowly soak in.

"The main thing for you to do is take it easy and recover, then we can go home." she said. They let Gunnar come in while she was still in there. "Look who's here," she said. She saw his eyes light up and he reached out his hand.

"I'm here Dad, I'm here," said Gunnar smiling through his tears. "You gave us quite a scare these last few days."

Coy flipped up his hand like it was nothing.

They laughed. His surgeon came into the happy room.

"Well Coy Danewood, I've been waiting to meet you," he said. "I'm Dr. James." Coy nodded his head slowly. "I have to poke and prod you just a little now to see how we did, putting you back together," the doctor said with a smile. He moved down to Coy's feet.

"He hasn't spoken," said Judith quietly standing next to the doctor.

"I have heard, we are about to change that," he said softly. "Tell me if you can feel this." He poked a dull needle into Coy's right arch.

Coy yelled out.

"Does that mean you felt it?"

"Yes, yes!" yelled Coy, "I felt it."

"Good," said the doctor winking at Judith.

"Now let's look at the rest of you," he said getting Coy to wiggle his toes and move his leg, then his fingers. "It is going to take time, but I predict Coy will make it all the way back to where he once was."

"How long?" Coy managed to get out.

"See that?" he asked Judith. "That's a man for you, we put him all back together and he wants to know how long he'll be here with us. To answer your question, as long as it takes. That's the only answer there is. I have to go, but first I want to hear you tell your wife how pretty she is today."

For the first time since he had woken up, his eyes softened and he said, "You are so pretty," and held out his right hand.

"Atta boy!" yelled the doctor who then

walked out.

Recovery was slow for the first two weeks. Coy was worried about his cows. He had made all the decisions for the ranch most of his life. Now here he was in a hospital bed not knowing what was going on at home. He would get Gunnar off by himself and ask him who was feeding them and how many bales they were putting out. Was he sure they had adequate water? What about minerals?

Gunnar started going home twice a week to check on everything. Word got around that he came home on Tuesdays and Saturdays and neighbors would come over and ask what they could do.

The teachers at Gunnar's school gave him lessons to work on while he was up at the hospital. On the second Saturday he was home, Jesse drove up in one of the McDaniel's Ranch pickups. She ran up and stood on her tip toes hugging him.

"I am so sorry," she said.

"Thank you," said Gunnar.

"How is he doing?"

"He's doing good, the doctor said about four or five more weeks and dad told me he's going to be out of there in two, if he has to break out."

"Really?"

"Oh yeah, that's my dad," said Gunnar proudly. "I have to go put out bags of loose minerals, want to come with me?"

"Is this a date?"

"It is for the cows," said Gunnar and they both laughed.

"I would love to help you feed minerals, Gunnar Danewood," she said. They had a great time together that afternoon talking about everything.

"How's your mother?" he asked smiling.

"My mother," she said. "I love her and sometimes I hate her, if that makes any sense," she said.

"Did you know my dad and her dated back in high school?"

She stepped close and grabbed his arm. "Really?" she asked.

"Yeah, I guess they parted badly and now there are hard feelings from your mom."

"Were they serious about each other?"

Gunnar realized he had said too much. "I don't know, maybe you should ask your mother."

When they got back, she said, "I have to hand it to you Gunnar, this was the most fun on any date I have gone on so far."

"Just how many dates have you been on so far?" he asked.

She came over and pulled him down and kissed him quickly on the lips. "One," she said then ran over to her truck laughing and drove away.

He drove back up to the hospital and told his father everything was fine at home. Coy wanted to know if Gunnar had counted the cows and what about the bill at the feed store. Judith told him she would mail a check from the hospital and all he had to think about was getting better. When Gunnar left, that next Tuesday,

Coy made sure no one could see him and held up two fingers. Silently he mouthed the words two weeks. Gunnar smiled until his jaws ached.

Next Saturday Jesse was at the ranch.

"We are going to have to quit meeting like this," Gunnar said.

It shocked her at first until she realized it was a joke. "I ought to just box your ears," she said.

"Go ahead if you think you can."

She came forward hitting him all over on his heavy clothes.

"Stop, stop," he yelled laughing. "I've already put out minerals, but we can go check the cows if you want to."

"That sounds even more exotic than last time," she said. This time she waited for him to open her door and smiled at him when he did. Once again, they spent hours together driving around and checking the cattle.

"Want to go into town and eat a hamburger?" he asked.

"I'd better not, someone will see us and tell my mother."

"Are you ashamed of me?"

"You know better than that. I just want to keep coming over here and having fun that's all."

"Okay," he said. This time he was ready when she pulled him down. He really kissed her for the first time.

"Wow, well Gunnar I'm going to have to watch out for you."

"Want another one?" he asked softly.

"I don't think I should."

"Your call," he said.

"I can tell from that look that right now is a good time for me to leave."

"Probably," he said.

He walked her to her truck and as she started it up, he took off his glove and touched her face.

"You are absolutely beautiful," he said leaving his hand on her face.

"My, my cowboy, you are way too good at this," she said before driving away.

He finished up everything and went to bed early. Sunday by noon he was back at the hospital telling his dad all about the cattle. The next Saturday he looked for Jesse all day, but she never showed. He drove over to Phil and Jean's house that night and asked if they heard any news about Jesse. He could tell that Jean was trying hard to keep from smiling.

"Only that a neighbor saw her driving away from the Danewood Ranch last Saturday and word got back to her mother who threw an absolute fit about it," she said.

"Oh," said Gunnar looking down.

"I wouldn't worry about it a whole lot," said Jean smiling. Gunnar looked down at the older woman. "These things have a way of working out."

He nodded and said, "I'm just glad she's okay."

"Uh huh," said Jean laughing.

Sunday when Gunnar walked into his dad's room he was greeted by a happy man and wife.

"Next Saturday I'm going home," his father said proudly. Gunnar looked over at his mother.

"The doctor said that he would see," she said.

"He can see all he wants, but I'm going home on Saturday," said Coy.

Gunnar could not stop smiling. That tough old father of his was going to make this happen. Saturday Gunnar was in the room when the doctor came in and sat down in a chair. He went over Coy's chart carefully reading all the pages. When the doctor looked up, Coy started speaking.

"I can see that doubt in your eyes doc, but don't ever doubt me. I'll do what you say, I give you my word. I'll do all these exercises and stretching that I have been doing here. I'll even walk farther if you want, but I need to leave here today. I have to leave here today."

The doctor slowly shook his head. "If half the people that come in here had your mental toughness my job would be so much easier. Will you go to the local hospital in Raton and get therapy?"

"Yes sir, three times a week," said Coy quickly. The doctor stood and looked at Judith and Gunnar.

"I don't know if you two know it, but that is a real man right there," he said pointing to Coy. He then walked forward and said, "Goodbye Coy, meeting you has been a real pleasure."

They stopped by the business office to check on the bill. The lady smiled and said it had already been taken care of.

"By who?" asked Coy.

"We don't know for sure," the lady said. "Some cowboy came in and paid your bill and said it was from a cowboy association of some kind. That's all any of us know."

"But who?" asked Coy sitting in the wheelchair.

"I'm sorry Mr. Danewood, it happened early yesterday morning and it is to remain anonymous."

Gunnar was pushing his dad toward the exit when Coy asked, "Now what cowboy association has that kind of money?"

Judith never said a word. It had to be in the hundreds of thousands of dollars.

Outside just before getting into the truck Coy said, "Glad we're driving, I'd never make it through the metal detectors at the airport." Judith laughed.

Coy took two pain pills on the way home. When they pulled in at the ranch, he said, "I never knew what a pretty sight this ranch is until now."

They got the truck close to the house and helped Coy get inside.

CHAPTER 5

Home

"I want to sleep on the couch tonight and wake up and see the sun on the mountains over there," said Coy looking out the big picture window, "That okay?" he asked Judith.

"Sure hon, anything you want," she said getting him set up on the couch.

"I am really tired," she said, "I missed my own bed so much. I'm going to go to bed. I'll leave my door open. If you need anything you just call out okay?"

"Okay sugar, you go on and get some sleep," said Coy.

Gunnar came over and kissed his father on his forehead. "You going to be all right here?"

he asked.

"'I'll be fine, now that I'm home."

"Okay I'll go to bed then. I'll leave the small kitchen light on."

Later that night, Coy watched his son bring in a blanket and lay back on the recliner in the living room. Tears rolled down Coy's face realizing his son was watching over him. He finally drifted off and woke in the early morning before daylight. He turned enough to see the digital clock over by the desk. It said 5:05. He called lightly to Gunnar who woke with a start.

"I need you to help me into the bathroom," he said.

"Sure," said Gunnar standing up.

"How do you want to do this?" he asked his Dad.

"Let me grab you around your neck with my right arm and we'll walk down the hall together."

"Okay," said Gunnar. He got his father into the bathroom and on the stool.

"You'd better leave, this isn't going to be very pleasant," said Coy grinning. Gunnar smiled and turned on the fan and closed the door.

"What's going on?" his mother asked from behind him.

"Oh," he said turning around. "Dad had to use the toilet that's all."

"Why is my door closed?" she asked.

"Because he told me to close it, that's why."

"He is so stubborn. I think I'll make him sit there for an hour," she said before going into the kitchen to make coffee. Gunnar came down the hall and looked in the kitchen.

"I need to use the bathroom in your bedroom," he said.

"Go ahead," she said, "everybody is using the bathroom this morning."

They got Coy out of the bathroom and back on the couch and Judith cooked breakfast. She was putting it on the table when Coy said, "There it is." She and Gunnar looked over to see the first rays of the sun hitting the tops of the mountains across the valley.

"This right here is what kept me going up there. Wanting to see this beautiful picture right here." Judith came over and sat with Coy. Gunnar came over and stood behind them.

"See how lucky we are," said Coy. She turned and looked at Coy and his casts.

"How many people get to see this every morning?" he asked. She put the palms of her hands on each side of his face and kissed him.

"I love you Coy Danewood," she said. "Now I'll bring you your breakfast."

Gunnar went back to school. All his friends were glad to hear his dad was home. He didn't see Jesse until lunch, when she sat right next to him.

"And how are you doing, Cowboy?" she asked.

"A lot better now," he said looking at her.

"You know, I got in a lot of trouble over you." she said.

"Was it worth it?"

"You can't ask me that."

"Sure, I can, was it worth it?"

She looked away and then back to him. "It was about half worth it," she said. "Tell me about your dad."

"He made it home like he said he would."

"But how is he?"

"His spirits are good, and he promised to do all his therapy. I think he'll recover. I cried a lot up there Jesse. I don't think we know how much we love our parents until we almost lose them."

"I guess," she said, "I sure get tired of my mother watching me like a hawk."

"Why do you think she does that?"

"I know what you're saying, but I could really use some slack." He smiled at her. "Don't look at me like that," she said. "It's true, she needs to lighten up on me." The bell rang and she said, "Good, I can't take much more of that smile."

"See you later," he said.

She turned back and said, "Maybe," then walked away laughing.

All the ranch work now fell on Gunnar. He started his day at 4:30 and was usually about thirty minutes late to school. He would drive straight home after school and chop holes in the ice so the cows would have plenty of water. If needed he put out more hay and fed the horses last thing using lights in the barn. His mother noticed he was grumpy. Slowly the days began to get longer and Coy got better.

Two weeks after he got home, they took the big cast off his leg and put on a small one where he could use his knee. Judith would watch his jaw muscles bulge and his face bead up with sweat when he did his therapy at the hospital. He was really concerned about his arm. They took the cast off two weeks later and put on a soft cast and a sling for him to wear. They gave him a rubber ball to squeeze three or four times a day. He squeezed that ball just about all the time. Judith had to take it away from him after the second day.

"They said twenty minutes four times a day," she said.

"Give it back. I have to do something," he snapped.

"Walk around some more, they said you could walk," she told him, shocked that he would talk to her like that.

"On a nice day I can drive you down to the road and you won't have to walk in the mud."

"Yeah okay, we'll do that," he said.

Two days later right after lunch he said, "I need to go for a walk on the road today."

"That would be fine," she said grabbing her truck keys. She got him out on the blacktop and off he went limping along headed west. She followed along in the pickup with her hazard lights on. After about twenty minutes she realized he wasn't stopping. She tapped the horn a few times, but he wouldn't stop. He waved back for her to stop the honking. She slowly went around him and stopped the truck in the road. She could see the sweat under his arms and under his neck.

"Okay Coy," she said, "fun's over get in the

truck."

"Since we are this close, I want to drive through the cows." She tilted her head to one side and squinted her eyes at him.

"Is this why you headed west?"

"It's where the cows are," he said bluntly.

"Okay, okay, we'll drive through the cows," she said.

Gunnar came home and Coy told his son all about driving through the cows and how they looked. Gunnar just smiled and listened. He saw the cows every day, most times twice a day.

Five mornings later Gunnar got up at 4:45, got dressed and walked into the living room to find his father up and waiting for him. He had what appeared to be a towel wrapped around the cast on his lower leg with a white trash bag taped over it.

"I'm going with you this morning," Coy announced. Then he said, "Coffee's ready."

Gunnar didn't say one word, he just went into the kitchen and got himself a cup of coffee then added milk to it. He looked around the living room and saw his dad's heavy outerwear.

"Been up long?" he asked quietly.

"Not quite an hour."

"There's no need to try and talk you out of this I guess?"

"No."

Gunnar sat quietly for a minute and then said, "She'll get mad."

"I know."

"Is it worth it for just a couple of weeks?"

"It is for me."

"She'll come down on me too you know."

"Yeah, but you're a big boy now," said Coy. "Start the truck and let it warm up a little."

"It's your call," said Gunnar before grabbing his coat and going outside. Coming back in Gunnar grabbed a pen and notepad. He was still writing when Coy asked, "What does it say?"

"That you're with me and you promised to be careful. You are going to be careful and stay in the truck, aren't you?"

"You bet"

"I mean it, I've never came down on you, but you're not going unless you give me your word you will stay in the truck."

Coy resented Gunnar talking to him like that. Where did he get off like that?

Coy held up his hand and said, "I, Coy Danewood, swear to stay in the truck, now can we get going?"

Shaking his head Gunnar said, "I see why mom gets so exasperated with you."

"Exasperated?"

"Never mind, just be careful going down the front steps," said Gunnar helping his dad.

An hour and a half later, Gunnar helped his dad back up the steps. She could hear them talking before they opened the front door. Coy limped into the house first and when Gunnar saw his mother's face, he was glad Coy was in front.

"Have a good time?" she asked through gritted teeth.

"You go and get ready for school," Coy told

his son. Gunnar walked down the hall keeping his head down.

"I need to talk to him too!" she yelled.

"You can, just let him get ready for school," said Coy. "I need to talk to you just as much as you need to yell at me." That surprised her. "I am not a complex person, I'm just a cow man. I like what I do and I'm good at it. I know this morning you don't believe it, but I'm no idiot. I can't sit around anymore. I have spent most of my life outside on the ranch working. I need to work, that's final. Now I will listen to what you have to say."

She sat there rocking back and forth not talking. Finally, she asked, "What did you do this morning?"

"Well we," he got out before she yelled "Not we, you! What did *you* do this morning?"

"First off, you watch your tone with me. I talked Gunnar into taking me along and just sat in the passenger side and watched Gunnar feed hay and chop two holes in the ice for the cows. Then we came home."

"Did you freeze your toes?" she asked calming down.

"No, I wrapped a towel around my cast and put a garbage bag around the whole thing."

"And you never put one foot out of the truck?"

"Nope, not one foot."

"Coy," she paused, "You are as hardheaded as an oak board," she said before getting up and going into the kitchen for another cup of coffee.

She stayed in there, drank some of her coffee and started cooking breakfast. That was the first time Coy ever talked that way to her, and it hurt. Gunnar came down the hall and looked over to his father. Coy still had that same look on his face.

"How many eggs do you want for breakfast Gunnar?" his mother asked.

"I don't eat breakfast on a school day," he said.

"Well you are today!" she yelled. Then calming back down she said, "Now then, how many eggs do you want?"

"Two," he said softly.

"Thank you, that's better," she said very politely. Gunnar looked over to his father who held up his hand, palm open and started shaking his head no, meaning don't ask any questions, just leave it alone.

By the time Gunnar brushed his teeth and was ready to leave, Judith was much better. She made him a sack lunch and handing it to him she asked, "Did he really just ride in the truck?"

"Yes, that's all he did."

"Okay," she said, "give me a kiss goodbye."

Her grown son pulled her to him, hugged her, then bent down and kissed her on her forehead. "Love you Mom," he said.

"I love you too," she said before he walked away.

"Okay Coy, what do you want for breakfast?" she called out. Coy got up and limped over to her. He wrapped his arms around her from behind.

"Careful, you're still on thin ice," she said. He gently rocked her back and forth. "I don't know what I would do if I lost you now. This whole thing scared me down to my core."

"I know Judith, I know," he said still rocking her gently.

"Just be careful, promise me that, be careful."

"I have to," Coy said. "Gunnar won't let me do anything yet."

"He's a good boy," she said.

"No, he's a fine young man now," said Coy.

She turned and hugged her husband and softly said, "Yes he is." She looked up at him and said, "Now nut job, go sit down and let me fix you breakfast."

"Deal!" he yelled out and limped away.

Coy started going out with Gunnar in the afternoons that day. She could see the difference in him immediately. He lost that frantic look in his eyes and thankfully was more like his old self.

CHAPTER 6

Haying Time

The first day of April, Coy told Gunnar to go to school and that from now on he and Judith would feed the cows. Gunnar was hesitant, but his mother nodded her head, so he agreed and went to school. On the first day of May the doctor took the cast off Coy's leg. His ankle was weak, so the physical therapist gave him a cane and showed him the way to slowly rotate his ankle in a circle while sitting down in a chair or on the couch.

From that day forward it seemed that Coy improved every day. When he wasn't working, he was practicing roping the dummy steer head. By June, he was walking without the cane and driving on the ranch. He asked Gunnar to go with him the first time he got on a horse to ride the BLM ground. Judith saw Coy saddling up two horses.

"It's a little soon," she said, Gunnar was standing there listening to every word.

"Probably," he said.

"But you're still going, aren't you?"

"Yes," he said, then turned and hugged her.

"I don't know why I put up with you."

"I do," he said getting on the horse on the right side instead of the left and slowly bringing his left leg over the saddle.

"Why?" she asked squinting up at him in the bright sunlight.

"My good looks," he said quickly and touched his heels to the horse making him start off with a jump.

Gunnar leaned down when he walked his horse by and smiling said to his mother, "That's my dad." They had a great day riding the BLM ground. Coy caught Gunnar looking at his watch.

"You have a plane to catch?"

"I was just getting hungry. Want to ride back in?"

Coy leaned back in the saddle, took off his hat and ran his fingers through his hair then put it back on. "You better hope you never have to lie about anything important son, because you are one terrible liar."

Gunnar turned his head and looked away from his father. He finally turned back and said, "It's been long enough for your first ride, let's go back to the house."

"That's better."

At the barn he had Gunnar help him get off the horse. Once he got down, he went over and sat on a short bench.

"I pushed it a little hard today," he told his son. "I'll take it easy for the rest of the day."

"Want me to bring the pickup down?"

"No, if you do, she won't let me on a horse for another year," Coy said. "How long were we out?"

"Almost two and a half hours."

"I'll rest up for three or four days then make sure I'm only on a horse for half that time. Do you mind riding the BLM ground on the west end tomorrow?"

"No, not at all."

Haying time was fast approaching, and Gunnar wondered about it. He caught his mother in the house while Coy was roping that dummy steer head and asked her what she thought about it. Together they came up with a plan for the two of them to cut and bale the hay.

Coy threw a fit when they told him. When Judith laughed, that made it worse. He finally went outside and sat on the front porch. Gunnar went outside and sat on the porch beside his father.

"I've been driving a tractor a long time," he said. Coy was silent. "I've done everything but run the baler. This might work out."

Coy looked over at him.

"My first bales probably won't be very pretty so this way I have a reason to learn how to make a decent bail. Don't you think I can do it?"

"Of course, you can do it, that's not it."

"Well what's got you so riled up?"

"Being useless, just sitting around breathing up good air and not really getting anything accomplished."

"Let me ask you, are the cows healthy?"

"Yes."

"Are the calves growing good?"

"Yes."

"Do you raise cattle here on the ranch?"

"Yes," said Coy starting to wonder where Gunnar was going with this.

"Well just what is it that you are doing so badly?"

Coy slowly shook his head and said, "I taught you too good son, way too good. Okay, I guess I'll be a haying consultant this year and just stand around and give advice. Heck, I might do that from now on."

"No, you won't Dad, you'll be lucky to sit this one year out."

"Probably," said Coy rubbing his son on the shoulder.

Coy stood and walked back in the house. "Are we still married?" he yelled out.

"I guess," she said hugging him with her head buried in his chest.

"Good," said Coy, "because I sure can't cook."

All three laughed. The three of them would work through the haying season together. Just like Gunnar predicted his first bales were not good at all, a lot taller on one side and not tight. He was trying as hard as he could. Coy walked out when he was half finished on the first field. He got Gunnar to stop the tractor and baler and let the motor slow down to an idle.

"Look at me son," he yelled over the noise. Gunnar leaned out of the cab and looked down at his father. "I wanted to see if one of your eyes was bigger than the other the way those bales look," he yelled. Then he threw back his head and laughed.

"How long did it take you to come up with that?"

"Over an hour," said Coy. "Want a little advice?"

"You bet," said Gunnar. Coy told him how he had done the same thing when he started and then gave him tips on how to build a better and tighter round bale. Gunnar was nodding his head as his father spoke. Coy ended with the words, "Anyway that's the way I do it, but it really doesn't matter. You'll get the hang of it by yourself."

Gunnar caught on and by the end of the season he was making tight round bales. Coy walked out when Gunnar was finishing the last small field. Gunnar saw him and put the tractor in neutral and climbed down and walked over.

"This was a terrible idea," said Coy.

"Oh?"

"Yeah, now you make a better bale than me. If your mother gets used to this, I'm really in trouble."

"Probably," said Gunnar mimicking his dad. They both laughed a while and then Gunnar heard his dad say softly, "Probably."

That night when Gunnar drove into town, Coy told Judith, "We have to do something special for Gunnar. He really stepped up to the plate this year."

"I agree," said Judith, "but what?"

"Let me work on that."

Sunday afternoon, Gunnar took his rifle out and shot at his 200-yard target. That gave Coy an idea. Tuesday morning, he told Gunnar to take the farm truck to school, he needed to check out something on Gunnar's pickup. When Gunnar came home there was a different truck in the yard. It was a kid's truck. It was newer than his, had a bright red paint job and big wide tires and rims on it. He walked in the house and asked his mother who was there.

"Just me and your dad," she said smiling.

Just then Coy came down the hall. He walked over and gave Gunnar a set of keys. "Here's the keys to your new truck, take it for a spin."

Gunnar kept looking from his dad to his mom. "Mine? That truck is mine?" he asked.

"Yep, you have been doing such a good job here on the ranch we wanted to do something nice for you," Coy said smiling.

Gunnar went out and looked the truck all over. It was awesome. He started it up and revved the motor. It sounded strong. He pulled out the drive and headed into town. He drove it to school the next day and all his friends gathered around giving him compliments on it.

Gunnar started shooting every third day. By the time the target shoot came up at Santa Fe, Gunnar was reloading his own ammunition. He noticed Jesse was getting a lot more popular and didn't come around him all that much. She yelled to him one day after school in the parking lot and he motioned for her to come over.

"I thought you forgot about me," was the first thing she said when they were close enough. He looked at her. "But I love your new truck."

"How could I forget you?" he asked.

"You haven't called or been to any school functions."

"I've been shooting a lot."

"Want to shoot a bottle off my head?"

"Not really," said Gunnar. "I called you over here to tell you I'll be going down to Santa Fe and I wanted to ask you to wish me luck."

"Okay, good luck."

"You're a hare brain."

"Want to kiss me?"

"I don't know, I'm kind of out of practice since you don't come out to the ranch anymore."

"I can't keep chasing after you."

"Why not?"

"I think I'm going to leave now," she said as she started to walk away.

"Throw me a kiss!" he yelled.

She puckered her lips, leaned forward and threw him a long kiss.

They picked up Phil and drove to Santa Fe. Gunnar was used to how everything went and took care of entering himself and finding out where to shoot. The men got him set up with Phil watching through the spotting scope for the 400-yard competition.

"Great," said Phil after the second shot.

Gunnar knew immediately after pulling the trigger on the third shot it didn't feel right. Phil didn't say one word. Gunnar chambered his fourth round and tried hard but now he was thinking about his last shot. After he shot, Phil never said a word. Coy didn't know what, but he knew something was wrong.

"Take your time son," he said.

The fifth and final shot felt better.

"That one fell right in there," said Phil.

When Gunnar got his target, he just dropped his head. When he got back to the bench the men had packed up the gear and were ready to leave. Gunnar gave his target to his father and climbed into the truck. Coy gave the target to Phil and started driving home.

"I'll bet you knew you shot poorly before you ever saw the target, didn't you?" asked Phil.

"Yes," said Gunnar through clenched teeth.

"You lost concentration for a moment and it cost you badly. Then it got to you and you shot badly again on the fourth shot. When you knew you had messed up and relaxed, the fifth shot fell right into the group." Gunnar didn't speak. "It can happen to anyone," said Phil.

Gunnar didn't talk for the rest of the way home. Coy and Phil talked but he sat in the back and sulked. At his house Phil got out of the truck then leaned back in.

"I know you are unhappy with yourself, but I'm glad this happened to you." Gunnar looked up quickly. "Today proved to you what happens when you lose concentration. Do you feel you are a better shot than that?"

"Yes," said Gunnar.

"Then you have to pull it back together. 400 yards is 400 yards, here, there, anywhere. What you can do at home you can do anywhere. Today proved you are a human not a machine. You think about that fifth shot and how easy it was. You knew you had nothing to lose and got back to just relaxing and letting it happen. That's where you want to be when you shoot." Then he said goodbye and closed his door.

They were not even out of town when Gunnar said, "I'm sorry Dad."

"What for?"

"For everything, for messing up shooting, just everything."

"None of us are perfect, son. Some of life's lessons are hard, but we need to learn them. What are you so upset about?"

"Here I am Gunnar Danewood, supposed to be such a great shot. Everyone knows that I shot well in the past, and I blow it."

"Did you lose an arm or a leg or die?"

"No," Gunnar said softly

"Then what's the big deal?"

"I just wanted to do better that's all."

"Who for?"

"Who for?" repeated Gunnar.

"Yeah, who is it you wanted to do better for?"

"Everyone I guess, I told some kids I was going down there to shoot."

"So, you're afraid of what some of the kids are going to say."

"Yeah."

"So, it's your pride that's hurting?"

"Yeah, I guess."

Sunday morning, they woke to find a note Gunnar left that said he had gotten up early and was riding the BLM ground behind the house. He rode back down and went into the barn just before 11 o'clock. Coy went down to see him.

"Well," said Gunnar as he took the saddle off his horse. "I've thought it through."

"And?"

"I missed the third shot and let it get to me."

"So, what's the end of this story?"

"I have to write this year off."

"Will you be ready and able next year?"

"You better believe I will!" said Gunnar.

CHAPTER 7

Darlene

A girl named Beth Snyder in Gunnar's class had a birthday party the ninth day of December and invited all her classmates to come. It fell on a Saturday and started at four in the afternoon. It was very evident to everyone at school that Jesse went to all kinds of parties and school functions. Gunnar decided to go to Beth's party and see if he liked it. He took the stairs down into the basement and found a room full of happy kids laughing and talking with music playing. Beth saw him and grabbed his arm. He smiled at her and said happy birthday. He was surprised when she kept hanging onto his arm and talking to the other kids.

Everyone turned and looked when Jesse came down the stairs with Bill Springer, the captain of the basketball team. He grew a lot last year and was now close to Gunnar's height. Jesse saw Beth hanging on Gunnar's arm and turned her head just a little and raised her eyebrows. The four said hello and made small talk. Then Beth let go of Gunnar's arm and asked Bill if he would like something to eat. She led him over to the table full of sandwiches, chips and soda.

"So, you're dating Bill now?"

"Yes, him and other boys that ask me out."

"Is he as good at kissing as I am?"

"Almost, want to kiss him and find out?"

"No, I'd just as soon not," said Gunnar laughing.

"I could ask you the same thing about Beth."

"Yes, but I wouldn't tell," said Gunnar rising to the challenge.

"Hey, hey," she said laughing, "serious Gunnar Danewood just made a joke. Here comes my date. I need to ask you something. Why don't you ever go to any school dances?"

"I don't know."

"Do you want to learn how to dance?"

"Are you offering?"

"Maybe," she said slipping her arm into Bill's who came back from the food table then walked away. Gunnar did what he always did and stayed in the background with some of the other kids. He tried to guess when they played charades that night. He watched the first boy and girl thank Beth and her mother for inviting them before they left. He was going to make sure he did the same thing.

He was thanking Beth and her mother for the invitation when he caught Jesse watching him. He gave Beth a light kiss on her cheek right in front of her mother and thanked them both. Beth acted embarrassed but squeezed his arm and smiled when she said good night.

The Danewoods had a nice Christmas and a great turkey dinner. Gunnar shot when he could but with winter coming, it was not often. Then the snow came. It was a long cold winter and they had snow cover one time for over seventy days straight. Coy was worried they would run out of hay, but they didn't. He told Gunnar in years like this you always wanted to save some of your best hay for last and feed some of the poorer quality hay while the snow was still on the ground and supplement it with cubes.

"That way," he said, "you have some good hay to slow them down in the spring when they get on the early grass and they won't get so loose."

One day at school they had a surprise safety drill. All the kids left the building in a safe and somewhat disorderly fashion. Jesse came over to him.

"My mother is always saying bad stuff about your parents, are they as bad as she says?"

Gunnar took a step back.

"My parents are good people. They are more respectful than most of the other kids' parents here."

"As far back as I can remember I have been told to stay away from them," said Jesse.

"Have you ever met them?"

"No."

"Maybe you should meet them and make up your own mind."

"How would I do that?"

"Ride your horse over some day. The days are now getting longer, pick a good one and ride over."

"I think I will," she said just before the bell rang for the kids to go back to class.

Saturday morning, he was in the barn when one of the horses knickered to a different horse and started acting up in his stall. He went outside and saw Jesse coming his way in the ditch along the side of the road in front of their place. He walked out to meet her.

"Good morning," he said when she was close.

"Good morning."

"Did you ride the ditch all the way here?"

"No, I came through our BLM lease down to the road."

"Isn't there a locked gate there at the road?"

"I have a key."

"Let's go up to the house."

"Sounds like a plan," said Jesse.

"So how are you going to scope out my mom and dad?"

"I will use some of my sleuth capabilities."

"I see," said Gunnar smiling and nodding his head.

Coy came out of the house and stopped cold

when he saw Jesse.

"Dad, can Jesse come into our house and meet Mom?"

"Sure, you bet," said Coy loosening up, "Please come in Jesse."

Judith recognized her from the rodeos. "Hello," she said, "I am Judith, Gunnar's mother, welcome to our home."

Jesse was surprised. The house was big and clean. Judith offered her hot chocolate and Jesse accepted. When Jesse had drunk most of it the conversation died down. Judith walked over and looked out the big picture window at Jesse's barrel horse.

"You have a beautiful horse."

"Yes, Buster is very handsome," the young girl said.

"Kind of like Gunnar," said Judith smiling.

The young girl never missed a beat. "Just like Gunnar," she said.

He didn't know what to do so Gunnar looked down. Judith winked at Jesse and the young girl liked that.

"Would you like to see my husband's rodeo buckles that he's won?" Judith asked.

"Yes, I would."

"Let's not make the poor girl suffer through that," said Coy. Judith looked over to Jesse.

"Lead the way," the young girl said. Judith was handing them to her one at a time when reflected light shone into the living room.

"Oops," said Jesse, "that's my mother."

Coy stood and walked over and watched Darlene McDaniels step out of her new four-door, four- wheel drive pickup in the yard.

"Maybe we should all go outside," he said.

Darlene stopped walking forward when she saw her daughter come out of the house followed by Gunnar then Coy then Judith.

"Just what do you think you're doing young lady?" she asked. She looked at Coy and said, "I guess you invited her here."

"I had no idea she was coming, but I enjoyed meeting her."

"Well that's great, just great. Jesse either get on your horse or get in this truck, you know you're not allowed over here."

"Why is that?" asked Judith stepping around Coy.

"One guess," said Darlene glaring at her.

Coy stepped forward and said "Don't do this Darlene. Don't let your anger and hard feelings for me boil over to these kids, they didn't do anything to deserve it."

He thought for a minute she might slap him, but she didn't. "I deserve all of the bad feelings you have for me, but they don't."

"Jesse!" Darlene called out, "Which way are you going to leave on your horse, or in the truck?"

"You just can't stay away, can you?" said Judith. "What's the matter Darlene, wasn't once enough for you?"

Darlene looked to Coy. He slowly lowered his head. Shaking her head, Darlene turned and motioned for Jesse to get in the truck.

The young girl walked over to Gunnar and gave him a quick kiss on the cheek.

"I'll see you later, handsome," she said. "Mr. Danewood," Jesse asked, "Can I leave Buster here until Spider can come over with the trailer and haul him home?"

"Absolutely," said Coy, "thank you for coming today."

"Coy," said Darlene standing by her truck, "You just don't see, I don't think you'll ever see," she said to him just before getting into her truck and driving away.

The three stood there in silence watching the mother and daughter leave in their pickup, then Coy walked down to the barn.

Judith watched Coy walking away and said to Gunnar, "You need to stay here."

Then she started for the barn. He was standing at the far end looking up at the mountains like he had before. He heard her walk in and turned to face her.

"How could you say that to her right in front of her daughter and our son?"

"I am fed up hearing about poor Darlene!" she yelled.

"What in the world are you talking about?"

"You always act like she is someone you have harmed. You make me feel I need to act the same way. Did you force yourself on her?"

"No."

"Then why are you always sticking up for her and not me?"

"I don't do that."

"Yes, you do, and I'm tired of it."

"Would you feel better if I hated her?" he yelled.

"Yes, as a matter of fact I would."

"Well, I don't and as for who was a bad example for our kids today, you were."

Calming down she said, "I'm going to ask you again, is Jesse your daughter?"

"No, I don't know how many times or ways I can say it, no she isn't."

"Well maybe I didn't behave very good today, but I am tired of hearing about her and seeing her. Can I come over to you now?"

"Not just yet, leave me be for a while."

"As you wish Coy Danewood," she said and walked back to the house.

She could see the look on Gunnar's face. "Sometimes married people have to clear the air about things," she said. "I know I haven't been friendly to Jesse in the past, but I didn't know her then. Now that I've met her, I like her." With that she turned and went in the house.

Jesse sat next to Gunnar before lunch was over on Monday. She had a pencil and she opened a spiral notebook and asked, "What was that all about at your house Saturday morning?"

"I'm not sure. I told you Dad dated your mother in high school."

"Was your mom jealous of my mother?"

"I don't know. I heard my folks talking it over down at the barn after you left."

"That's kind of different," she said.

"For sure," he said.

"I need your address," she said.

He gave it to her and waited as she wrote it

down. "How come you want it?" he asked.

She kissed him on the cheek and said, "You'll find out."

Things began to get back to normal and Coy noticed that Gunnar took more interest in roping, so they started practicing more in the small arena there at the ranch. Coy was careful not to put too much pressure on his left arm. Being young, Gunnar's ability came back quickly.

Judith showed them the thank you letter Jesse sent, saying how nice it had been being invited into her home and how she had really enjoyed meeting her. She surprised them both by taping it on the refrigerator door.

The school year ended and Coy told Gunnar that if they got the haying equipment ready to go early, they could fit in a trip up to Durango for the rodeo before they started haying. Gunnar wanted a chance to win some more money. He and Coy would watch a new video Coy had of world champion Team Ropers. Gunnar then tried his best to adapt his style of heeling to the way the champions did it on the video. Coy could see the improvement right away.

The men were packing up and getting ready to go when Judith told them she wasn't going to go. Her back had been bothering her for several days and she thought she would stay home and rest. Coy was torn between wanting to take Gunnar to the rodeo and staying home with his wife.

"Gunnar practiced and is all ready to go. I'm

not going to let him miss his opportunity just because I have a little pain," she said. She could see the concern in her husband's eyes. "I'll be fine. You take Gunnar up to Durango and win some money and I'll be right here when you get back." He didn't say a word. "If you're thinking of telling Gunnar you should back out and stay here, don't because that will make me go and I'll be more comfortable here just taking it easy laying around."

"I'll agree to go, but you keep that phone right beside you and call me if you start feeling worse. There will always be another rodeo," he said.

"I'll keep the phone right beside me."

"Even at night," he demanded.

She motioned for him to come over to her. He bent down by her where she was sitting in her rocking chair. She pulled him close, kissed him on the side of his face and said, "Even at night, now you take our son to the rodeo."

He didn't like it, but he went ahead and took Gunnar up to Durango.

He called her as soon as they got to the rodeo grounds. It was obvious he woke her up. He apologized and told her to go back to sleep. They were warming up their horses in the arena when a woman rode by and looked back at Coy. Gunnar saw her blonde hair under her cowboy hat and looked over at his father.

"You know her?"

"I don't think so," said Coy.

The next time she rode by she was close and pulled her horse up to a walk and turned to look at Coy. She was smiling when she asked, "Are you Coy?"

"Yes."

"Coy from New Mexico?"

"Yes."

"Well Coy, I'm Rita from Valentine, Nebraska," she said showing pretty teeth. Coy was surprised. "Is this your son?"

"Yes, this is my son Gunnar."

"You sure got busy when you got home didn't you?"

"I did, how about you, are you married?"

"Not anymore."

"Do you have children?"

"Nope, all I have are my horses that I love."

Coy nodded. He looked down for a minute and then looked back up. "How is your uncle, is he here?"

She threw her head back and laughed loudly. Getting control, she said, "No he doesn't go with me anymore. He won't be giving you any trouble this time. Listen, look me up after the rodeo and we'll go get a drink or something." Coy nodded his head then she galloped away.

"Well, well, Dad," said Gunnar, with a big smile.

"We met when we were kids down in Texas at a rodeo. Her uncle hated my guts."

"Were you two serious?"

Coy laughed and said, "No, she was as wild as the wind and it appears still is, but no we just met and talked at a rodeo."

"I think she wants to see you tonight."

"I'm going to tell you something about life

right now son, wanting and getting are two very separate things." Gunnar laughed. "Now I say let's win some money and go home."

They got bumped down to second place by the third to last team. They stuck around long enough to pick up the $1600 and headed home. Gunnar started driving and Coy slept.

At one in the morning Gunnar woke his dad and said, "You better take over, I nodded off just a minute ago." Coy drove the rest of the way home and together they unloaded the horses, fed them and put up their gear.

Coy tried to be quiet getting into bed but Judith woke and asked how they did. "We took second and won $1600," he said.

"That's good, I'm going back to sleep," she said turning over on her side.

Both men slept in the next morning and didn't get up until 8 o'clock. Coy was shocked when he came in the kitchen and saw Judith that morning. She had dark circles under her eyes, and she looked like she didn't eat while they were gone.

He knelt beside her. "Are you all right?" he asked softly.

CHAPTER 8

We Don't Need One

"I don't know, I think maybe I should go see a doctor," she said. He didn't hesitate, he walked down the hall and knocked on Gunnar's door.

"I'm awake," said Gunnar.

"Your mother isn't feeling good. I'm taking her into town. You do the morning chores okay?"

Gunnar came to the door in his underwear. "Sure Dad," he said.

Coy drove the pickup up to the front steps.

"You had better call for an appointment," Judith said.

"We don't need one, come on now, let's go," he said helping her into the truck.

He drove her to the emergency entrance of the small hospital in Raton and she refused to go in.

"Hon, you look pretty rough, let's just get you in here and see what's going on," he said.

She finally let him help her out of the truck and went into the hospital. They put her in a room and a doctor came in and examined her.

He smiled and said, "Now we are going to pull some blood and take some x-rays." He asked Coy to follow him out into the hall. Outside he said, "She is definitely ill. We won't know until we run some test, but she has a serious problem."

Coy went back in her room and tried to act like nothing was wrong.

"Coy, you are terrible at trying to hide something. No secrets, what did he say?"

She saw his expression change to a serious one. "He just told me you were seriously ill."

Nodding her head, she said, "I thought so, I've never felt this bad before."

"I'm going to call Gunnar," he said.

She nodded her head yes but didn't speak. Gunnar got the message and came into town. He walked into her room and kissed his mother.

"Do we know anything yet?" he asked.

"No, we're just waiting," said Coy.

The doctor came back in with an x-ray and put it up on a screen. He didn't turn the light on but turned and looked at each one for a moment then over at Judith.

"You have a serious problem. This is going to

be a shock."

She slowly nodded her head and said, "Go ahead and show us the x-ray."

He flipped the switch that illuminated the x-ray.

"See this large organ right here?" he said, "This is your pancreas. It is not supposed to look like this." He turned to face her. "Your bloodwork shows that your body is really fighting something."

"Is it cancer?" she asked.

"We would have to run more tests to be sure, but I believe it is."

"What should we do?" asked Coy.

"If she were my wife, I would take her to Santa Fe today and admit her into the Hospital down there. They have an up to date oncology program down there."

"Oncology?" asked Gunnar.

"It's a cancer treatment center," said Judith quietly. Gunnar felt like the bottom fell out of his stomach.

"How far along is the cancer?" he heard his mother ask.

"There is no way to tell from the test we have run, but you have had this for a while."

"We better get you checked out and down to Santa Fe" said Coy. The doctor nodded his head and left the room. They dressed her and wheeled her outside and into Coy's pickup. Judith held up her hand before Coy started the truck.

"Should Gunnar stay here?" she asked. Coy looked at her.

"There are chores to be done and animals to be fed, maybe he should stay here and let us call him from down there."

"I'm going" said Gunnar.

"Okay, but you drive your truck and follow us. If I stay, you can drive back and take care of everything" said Coy.

"Okay," said Gunnar climbing out of his dad's truck.

They admitted Judith into the hospital in Santa Fe and met the cancer doctor. He looked at the x-ray they had brought and read some of the bloodwork that had been done. He didn't say anything for a moment, being deep in thought.

"There are a couple of ways we can go here," he said. All three people stared at him. "I think the best thing to do is to take a biopsy this afternoon to make sure, but I do believe it is cancer. I suggest starting chemotherapy just as soon as we find out."

"When will you take the biopsy?" Judith asked.

The doctor looked at his watch and said, "Probably in about an hour. The biopsy is going to really hurt." He looked over at the father and son and said, "You two can't be there when they take it."

"Okay," said Coy. Gunnar said okay but much softer thinking how much it would hurt his mother.

"Gunnar, I need you to step outside for a moment," said Judith. When he was out the door, she motioned for Coy to close the door.

"Coy," she said, "We need to talk. I'm probably not going to survive this, and I need you to tell me you're going to be okay."

He went over and sat in a chair. How did this happen? he wondered. Was it from her early life? Maybe there was some mistake. He looked up at her. No, this wasn't a mistake, she was very ill.

"I'm serious now, I need you to tell me right now that you're going to be okay." He shook his head no for a minute then stood and came over to her and his eyes filled with tears.

"I can't, I can't tell you that," he said then bent down and put his face by hers and cried.

She hugged him and through her tears she said, "I love you so much Coy." He managed to get out that he loved her too. Then she said, "We can't let Gunnar see us fall apart like this."

Standing up he said, "I guess not."

Gunnar could tell they had both been crying. All three made small talk until the nurses came and took Judith for the biopsy. When they wheeled her back in, she looked rough. She was slow getting into her bed. She told her nurse as soon as she laid down that she would like her pain pill. After about ten minutes Coy was getting aggravated. Finally, the same nurse came back in with the pill.

"This will probably put her to sleep," she told Coy. Judith was getting drowsy within minutes, so she told Gunnar to drive careful and go on home to the ranch. He looked over to his father.

"You should probably go and call the

neighbors and let them know what's going on. We might need their help later."

Gunnar said okay and went over to his mother's side. "Love you Mom," he said holding out his hand.

"I love you too, son," she said taking his hand. "Now you be careful driving home." Gunnar walked slowly down the hall and outside to his truck.

Coy had been brought up right and knew what he should do. Late that night he got down on his knees by her bed and started to pray. Through his tears he began to bargain with God. Then realizing what he had done he did better. He prayed that Gunnar would be safe, and that Judith would get through this. He finally said amen, took out his handkerchief and wiped his eyes and slowly stood up.

"That was beautiful," Judith said softly.

He laid his upper body on her bed. "Are you feeling any better?" he asked.

"I feel better after hearing you pray for me. I never knew you were religious," she said reaching for his hand.

"I hadn't thought about it for years until this happened," he said. "Mom and Dad made sure I went to church when I was a boy, I guess it stuck."

"Good," said Judith, "you're going to need it to get through this. Can you sleep in that chair over there?"

"Maybe, I don't know."

"Well you need to, because I want to go back to sleep."

He softly kissed her hand and said, "You go back to sleep."

His praying helped him. He sat in the chair and finally went to sleep. He managed to get in three hours before the nurses of the early morning shift change woke him up. He looked out the big window and saw that it was still dark. He got up and went closer to the big clock on the wall.

It was 4:55 and he had to find a bathroom. He used the one down the hall. When he opened her door, the lights were on and a nurse was taking Judith's blood pressure. He walked over and held her hand. The nurse finished and said, "Your doctor is on the floor and will be in soon."

She wasn't out of the room when Coy asked, "How are you this morning?"

"About the same," said Judith. They brought her food tray and the young woman put it on the big table that rolled over and across her bed.

"Have you eaten?" Judith asked. He looked at her. "I didn't think so, eat some of mine," she said.

Coy finally smiled, "I will if you will," he said. As bad as she felt she couldn't help it, she had to smile. Coy was her man and she was his woman. He wasn't going to eat until she did.

"I'm too weak to argue with you," she said and picked up a piece of toast. He fed her some oatmeal and ate a little himself then they shared the one cup of coffee.

"That wasn't much, want me to go get you

some more?" he asked. She didn't answer because the doctor came in.

"You two seem to be strong people. This is hard news so I'm going to lay it right out." Judith was nodding her head but Coy was barely breathing. "The cancer you have is very aggressive. It has already spread to other parts of your body. It is what we call stage four. There is only one option, we start chemotherapy and watch to see how your body responds. If we caught this sooner, it would have been better."

"Do you think the chemotherapy will cure me?" she asked.

He paused and looked at her. "We never know how a specific cancer will respond to treatment," he said. She just kept looking at him. "Your cancer is pretty far advanced," he finally said softly.

"Thank you for the truth."

"We will start your treatments today and I will tell you they are going to be pretty rough as weak as you are. Try to eat all you can. We will give it to you intravenously and want you to stay here overnight. We will give you pills to take at home then you can come back in three weeks and we will take more x-rays and see how you are doing. We will also give you pain medication for your time at home." Then he gave them each a small smile and left the room.

"Close the door," she said softly after the doctor left. Coy walked over and did as she asked. "Now come over and sit on my bed," she said patting the side of her bed. She started just as soon as he sat down. "I need you to give me your word you are going to keep it together if I don't make it." He felt his shoulders slump as his gaze fell to the floor. "Gunnar isn't even 18 yet and he's going to need a strong person to help him get through this."

"You're talking like you've already accepted it. You have to fight this thing."

"I'll fight, you can bet on that, but I want to talk about this while my mind is good and clear. I want to live but I might not have the choice. You are a kind, caring person that loves me too much. If I don't make it, I need to know you are going to keep it together and raise our son."

"I don't want to think about life without you."

"I know, but you have to think about Gunnar. Now you give me your word, you promise me if things go south, I can count on you."

He finally looked up and said, "I give you my word I'll do all I can to see Gunnar grows up right."

"Good, I'm glad we got that taken care of. I'll have more to say later but you just know that I love you with all my heart."

"I know that Sugar, I know."

"I think I'll try to sleep now," she said getting comfortable in her bed.

The doctor set the time for her to receive the chemo for two o'clock in the afternoon so she would have time to digest her lunch before the drug really hit her. She felt bad and weak from the chemo but kept her food down.

Coy called Gunnar that afternoon and told him they would be coming home the next day so he might as well stay home. When he asked Coy about how the chemo affected his mother ,Coy told him that it hit her pretty hard.

Coy checked her out and brought her home the next day. He was so down he couldn't hardly even raise his head up. When Gunnar saw the look on his dad's face, he knew how serious everything was. Judith was the only one not almost in tears. Inside the house after she had taken a nap, she asked her son, "Gunnar can you cook?" It shocked him.

"I don't know, I've really never tried."

"Well I want you to learn because I think that if this cancer doesn't kill me your father's cooking might." Coy looked up with a half-smile.

"You two get in the kitchen and do what I tell you. Gunnar, you peel about four average size potatoes. Wash them first and again after they are peeled. Coy, you get a package of hamburger out of the freezer. I'm going to teach you both how to cook," she said.

Her attitude set the pattern for the next three weeks. They spent every minute they could together when she wasn't sleeping. To Coy it only seemed like a little over a week until they drove back down to Santa Fe for a one o'clock appointment at the hospital.

They admitted her and took an x-ray that afternoon. The doctor came in the next morning. He had two x-rays that he put up on the screen in her room. "I have some news and it's not good," he said quietly. He flipped the switch that turned on the light on the screen. He pointed to the first x-ray and said, "This is the first x-ray." Pointing to the second he said, "This one is yesterday's x-ray. It's hard for an average person to see but the pancreas shows more cancer." Coy felt the bottom fall out of his chest and stomach. He slowly looked over to the doctor. "Unfortunately, this means the chemo had no effect, it is still progressing."

"Surely there is some other treatment or something we can do," said Coy.

"I'm afraid there isn't, the cancer was too far along before we found it."

"How long?" asked Judith. Coy snapped his head over to look at her.

"I can't say for sure," said the doctor.

"I understand, I need to know what to expect, give me an estimate of time and how I will feel."

"My guess is ten to twelve weeks. The pain will get worse and you will get much weaker towards the end. If you take enough medication to relieve the pain, you will sleep most of the time close to the end."

Coy hadn't taken his eyes off Judith. She was slowly nodding her head that she understood.

"I really wish I had better news," he said then turned and left the room.

"Coy," she said, "Let's get my prescription and go home."

Coy felt hollow driving home. He even drove slowly. She spoke after they were on the road for about thirty minutes.

"I knew this would work out this way." He kept driving. "I've heard about people having a feeling, but somewhere deep down inside me, from our first trip to the hospital, I knew how this would end. I'm going to hold you to your word, Coy. You promised me you would keep it together and make sure Gunnar makes it through all of this."

Slowly and deliberately Coy nodded his head yes.

"This will be a big load for you to carry, but you have to carry it." Coy slowly nodded his head again.

"Let's stop at the cafe for pie and ice cream, I don't have to watch my weight anymore."

He looked over and she winked at him. He smiled a little.

"I knew I could get a smile out of you. Maybe I'll come over there and push you like you pushed me that day in front of the woman's clothing store, do you remember?"

He nodded his head and said, "I remember."

"This is what I want, this is what I need, this right here, you and me laughing and remembering. According to the doctor at the end I will be heavily sedated so it's important that I enjoy what time I have. Can you see that?" He didn't answer right away.

Finally, he said, "I can see what you are saying, but I don't know if I can do that. I am losing the love of my life, my best friend, the mother of my son. How can I be happy?"

"Okay, I hear you Coy. I'll make you a deal, you be sad and cry all you want after I'm gone but you try to be happy while I'm still here okay?"

"You always amazed me and still do, where do you get that steel you're made of?"

"Maybe from my Irish ancestors," she said, "What do you think?"

He slowly began to come around just a little and said, "Maybe."

"Right now, I'm going to lay my head on your lap and sleep until I get home so I can be rested when I speak to Gunnar."

Coy drove home either stroking her hair or resting his hand on her shoulder. He woke her just south of Raton.

"Do you really want pie and ice cream?" he asked. She sat up slowly and looked over at him with a sleepy expression.

"No, I was just messing with you. I'm glad you woke me up though, I need to be wide awake when I talk to Gunnar. Are you getting adjusted to what's ahead of us?"

"I guess the shock has worn off, now the certainty is bearing down on me."

She kept looking at him.

"I promise you I will do the best I can, but that's all I can do."

She reached up and touched his face "That should be enough my love."

Gunnar came out when they drove up to the house.

"I will need to talk to him alone," she said.

He helped her to the front porch, and she sat

on one of the chairs they had there.

"What did the doctor say?" Gunnar asked.

"I'm going down to check on the horses," said Coy before slowly walking away.

"Well?" Gunnar asked.

"Sit down beside me," Judith said.

Coy stayed down at the barn for at least twenty minutes. He walked back to the open barn doors and looked up at the house. No one was on the porch, so he walked up and went inside. He found Gunnar sitting beside his mother on the couch holding her hand.

"Gunnar knows everything we know," said Judith. "I think it will help as we go forward. I have a few requests," she said.

Coy walked over, knelt, and said, "Anything Judith."

"I want to watch you two team rope at least two more times. I enjoy seeing you two doing that so much, but I don't think I can run the chute. I also want you to let me go with you when we check the cattle in the old flatbed."

Gunnar was nodding his head and said, "Okay."

"And I will ask you to invite special people to come out to our home."

"Okay," said Coy, "what else?"

"Those are the main things. I will need paper and envelopes so I can write down some thoughts."

"Sure," said Coy, "anything else you want you just tell us."

"I think we should do the outside stuff first, don't you?"

"Yes, we'll do those first," he said. "Is there anyone in your past you want to contact?"

"No, my life came to be after I met you. My real life all happened here."

Coy couldn't sleep. He finally drifted off and slept in until 7:30. He found Gunnar in the kitchen drinking coffee. It was easy to see that he hadn't slept much either. He motioned for his son to join him outside on the porch. He told him from then on, he thought they should drink their coffee outside on the porch and talk out there to let Judith sleep.

"If she doesn't wake up by nine o'clock, I think you should go up to the Jenkins and ask if their son can come down and run the chute for us to rope. Tell the boy it's worth $20.00 in front of his parents. That way they can't make him do it for free, when they hear the news."

After that they sat on the porch each with his own thoughts. She interrupted their thoughts by opening the front door and stepping out.

"What are you two doing out here? Scheming and planning stuff so I won't hear you?" She saw Coy's facial expression change from concern to a little smile.

"You've always been ahead of me, ever since the first day that I met you."

"I'm a wife, that's what we do, now tell me your guys' big plans."

Gunnar smiled watching his dad confess to their plans of talking outside and asking the Jenkins boy to run the chute. The love his parents had for each other seemed to shine out of them. Her words brought him back to their conversation.

"We will have to do it early and have the horses taken care of by 10:30," she said. Coy looked over to Gunnar then back to Judith.

CHAPTER 9

Quit Shaking Your Head

"Why 10:30?" he asked.

"Because by then you'll be driving the haying equipment out into the fields," she said. Coy stood and started shaking his head no.

"I won't have it," he said. "I won't have us out there on tractors and you up here sick in the house!"

"Sit down and quit shaking your head Coy, you lost this argument when it started. The world won't stop turning because I have cancer. You've already turned the bulls back into the cows. When you sell calves this fall they will already be carrying next year's babies. They are going to need hay for this winter. Like you have told me so many times, this is what we do, we, our family, this is what we do. The verdict is already in and we put up hay again this year just like always."

"Judith," he said.

"Now you stop that right now, I have never seen you beg, and I don't want to now." She took a deep breath and said, "Now be a good husband and get me another cup of coffee." Coy let out a sigh ,walked up and took her cup and went into the house.

"Did you see what happened?" she asked Gunnar.

"Yes."

"That is how women handle our men. You need to learn that. I make Coy do my wishes because he loves me so much. I'm going to want you to bring Jesse to come see me pretty soon."

"Jesse?"

"Yes, she's the only young person I know, and I like her."

"Okay Mom, whatever you want."

Coy came back out with their coffee.

"There's something else I want you to buy me," she said taking her coffee cup.

"Okay," said Coy.

"I want a diamond necklace about the size of a ripe plum." The men just looked at each other. Then she burst out laughing. Wiping her eyes, she said, "This is so much fun. You should see your faces. Can't you tell I'm just messing with you?" Coy shook his head and looked off towards the mountains. "Come over here and sit by me Sugar," she said to her husband. He came over still shaking his head and sat next to her. "I want you to buy me one of those four-wheel drive side by side little buggies. That way I can drive out to see you guys."

Very concerned he asked her, "Are you sure?"

She didn't answer for a second or two then with a big smile she asked, "Does a bear crap in the woods?" Coy put his arms around her and hugged her.

"Yes Judith, I believe a bear does crap in the woods. We'll get you your buggy."

Then they sat there enjoying their morning coffee. Later she told Coy that he better watch the weather because when it rained them out of putting up hay, he could take the flatbed trailer and go buy her that four-wheel drive buggy.

Later she told him she wanted him to go into town to the feed store and get Jean by herself. She told him to tell her that she was ill and needed to see her and to make it tomorrow evening if possible. The next day he bought baler twine and got Jean off to the side and told her Judith's wishes. She wanted to know what was wrong. He told her that Judith was seriously ill.

Jean showed up at 6:30 that evening. The men stayed outside. Jean came to Judith and saw how thin and pale she was. Judith told her she had cancer and Jean's hand went immediately to her mouth.

"It was too far along before we found it and Jean," she paused, then added, "I won't be here much longer." She saw Jean clench her teeth. Then she began to blink her eyes as the tears filled them. "I wanted to thank you for everything you have done." Jean dropped her head. "You have been closer to me and mean more to me than my mother ever has. You melted my heart when you gave me your mother's rolling pin. Next to Gunnar and Coy it is my most prized possession. I am very weak now and can't talk very long, but I wanted to see you, thank you, and tell you I love you before it's too late."

Jean tried to talk but couldn't. She was crying and looking down. She got control enough to try and said, "You shouldn't be thanking me, I should be thanking you for the privilege of knowing you. You have always been so truthful, so straight forward and in today's world I don't see that very much."

They hugged each other, cried some more, then Judith told Jean she needed to lay down. The last vision of Jean, Judith had, was her looking back at her with her handkerchief covering her mouth.

It was getting close to sundown when Jean came back outside. She came out and hugged Coy and started to cry but caught herself.

She stepped back and wiped her eyes and said, "I am older than either one of you. I am supposed to know what to say at a time like this, but I don't. I just don't. Coy, Gunnar, I am so sorry." She started crying then went over to her car and drove away.

When they went inside, Judith was drying

her eyes with a Kleenex.

"Besides you two, Jean is the best friend I have. I had to thank her for everything she has done."

Judith went over and laid down on the couch. Coy got Gunnar outside and told him to go get the Jenkins boy lined up for tomorrow morning at eight o'clock. Then he walked down to the machine shed and looked at the swather. He had to come up with a way to make the haying go faster. Standing there he came up with a couple of good ideas. He went back in and checked on Judith and found her fast asleep on the couch.

The next morning, Judith could hear cattle bawling. She saw the men had the cattle brought down to the pens. They were sorting out the roping steers. She got a cup of coffee and watched and when they had the last steer out of the herd, Gunnar got off his horse and left in the pickup. Coy drove the steers into the roping arena, shut the gate and rode his horse up to the house.

Opening the front door quietly he was greeted by his wife.

"Hello cowboy," she said smiling.

He walked over and took her hand, "How do you feel this morning?" he asked.

"With my hands mostly," she said smiling.

He nodded his head and smiled at her. "Do you feel up to watching us rope this morning?" She turned her head just a little and smiled. "Don't you say it," he said, "I can tell by that grin what you're thinking about saying." She hugged him and put her head sideways against his chest.

"Yes, I feel up to that," she said.

Even though the sun was out, and it was warm, they bundled Judith up and put her in a chair about halfway down the side of the arena. The Jenkins boy did a good job running the chute and they roped the steers for almost two hours. Coy said something to Gunnar then tied his horse on the fence by the gate and came over to Judith. She saw Gunnar and the Jenkins boy go over to the pickup and drive away.

"Party's over," said Coy, "Let's get you back in the house." He noticed how slow she got up and her hands were cold when he touched them. "Let's go get warmed up ,I'm a little cold," he said.

On the porch before going in, she asked, "Do you think I'm really buying this, you cold on a warm day like today?"

"We still need to get you in the house."

He made her hot chocolate. He went over and stood by the window looking outside.

"You need to start today," she said. He looked down then turned around. "The sooner you start, the sooner you finish, quit worrying about it and just go make it happen."

"You're still ahead of me," he said, "Like always."

"I'm your wife," she said, "That's my job. Did you guys eat this morning?"

"No, we got the cattle up first thing."

"Then you better fix both of you a big

breakfast."

He looked over at the wall clock and saw it was 10:45. A big breakfast could hold them until late in the afternoon. As they were eating ,Coy laid out his plans. They would start down at the west end like always and work their way east. He told Gunnar that today he would start cutting and Gunnar could stay with his mother.

"We are going to need one of those new moisture testers from the feed store to speed things up," he said. "You need to go buy one today. If Mom feels up to a ride, she can go with you."

"No," said Judith, "Gunnar you go. I'll stay here."

"Okay," said Coy, "You follow me down on the highway, so no one runs over me, and after I get started you beat it to town and buy the moisture tester."

Inside the gate down on the west end Coy told Gunnar to stick around until he got started and make sure he didn't have a problem. He put the swather in gear and away he went. Gunnar stayed until he was halfway around the field then Coy waved real big and Gunnar headed for town. Coy finished the first round and as he started the next one, he put the swather in the next higher gear. He didn't have near the control and it was a rough ride, but the machine was cutting the hay. His first idea was working.

Gunnar came out to him that afternoon. Coy had finished the first field and was over halfway through the second one. He handed his father a sandwich and said, "You are bouncing all over that thing."

"Don't I know it."

"You look like you're ahead of last year already."

"I know," said Coy walking back and forth stretching out his legs.

"Think the machine will hold up?"

"I don't know, but I'm going to stick with it. The sooner we finish the more time we have with your mother."

They got rained out on the fourth day. Judith got up and found Gunnar drinking coffee, he pushed the note over to her. It said that Coy took the flatbed trailer and went down to Santa Fe to buy her a side by side four-wheel buggy. He was back that afternoon and unloaded the small rig and drove it up to the house. She was waiting on the front porch as he drove up.

"Here you go Sugar," he said. "It's not a diamond necklace, but it should take you anywhere you want to go."

She drove it around with Coy as a passenger and they laughed at her driving. It had so much traction it would push forward as she tried to make a turn. She tore up some grass in the front yard.

Later she asked how the hay was going and Coy told her, "Pretty good really, we are definitely ahead of last year." He caught her watching him out of the corner of his eye, but acted like nothing was wrong.

Judith rode her buggy out to watch Coy cut

hay the next morning. She hid behind some trees in her buggy close to the northeast corner of the large field to surprise him. Her mouth came open when he drove the swather by and barely made the turn. She couldn't believe what she saw. She started her little rig, drove over and opened the gate, then parked it right in the middle of his next pass. He saw her up there and got the swather stopped in plenty of time. He could tell she was mad the way she was standing.

"What do you think you are doing?" she asked.

He put his gloved hands on his hips and looked around. "On a guess I would say I was cutting hay in a hayfield."

"You are going to tear that machine up driving like that!" she yelled. He looked down and tapped the toe of his boot on something in the ground.

"Say something, Coy Danewood!"

"It's worth it," he said calmly looking up. That wasn't what she had expected.

"What do you mean?"

"I think we can get the hay put up six or seven days faster than last year."

"And that is worth tearing up the swather?"

"It would be worth it to spend one more hour with you."

She shook her head and turned away. He walked up behind her and hugged her gently.

"Oh Coy, you are something."

"I am your husband and I want all the time with you I can get." Still looking away she just shook her head.

"Right now, I'm going to ask you to move your buggy so I can get going again."

She turned around and told him to be careful.

"I am," he said, "I swing wide on the turns after I get the first two rounds made. We are flat making it happen out here." She slowly walked to her little buggy and heard Coy raise the RPMs on the swather. When he drove by, he whipped off his hat and yelled, "Yippee!"

She went up and sat on the front porch. The men finished the hay in seven more days using the new moisture tester. It enabled them to start baling earlier and bale an extra hour longer in the evenings. She told Gunnar the day they quit baling to call Jesse and see if she would come over the next day right after lunch.

Judith was surprised when Jesse drove in at 11:30. "Good girl," she said softly and opened the front door before Jesse quit knocking. "Jessie," she said, "please come in."

She saw the shock on Jesse's face. Jesse was instantly serious and asked, "Ma'am, are you all right?"

"Please come sit on the couch with me."

Wasting no time, she started right in, "I like you Jesse, you have spirit, you think for yourself and you are very bright. I asked Gunnar to have you come over because I'm very ill and will not live very long." Jesse put her hand up to her mouth like she had lost her breath. "I want to tell you some things I had to learn the hard way. My time is short, and I feel the need to leave this with a younger woman." Jesse slowly nodded her head. "This has nothing to do with Gunnar unless you decide to make it so."

Jesse came forward, hugged Judith and cried, when they were finished. Judith wiped the tears away from her own eyes and said, "See, I knew I liked you."

Jesse finally pulled herself together and quit crying. They tried to make small talk, but Judith knew it was time.

"I'm sorry but I am very tired, I'm afraid I have to lie down and sleep now." Jesse was polite and said she understood, then said goodbye.

CHAPTER 10

Thank You

S he knew she was getting weaker. The next morning, she waited until the men were getting ready to go to the hayfield and bring in the equipment. She told Coy to go on, she wanted a minute with Gunnar. She held out her hand to him and he came over and sat down beside her.

"There are some things you need to know. By now I'm sure you've heard the stories of your father branding that man down by the barn." Gunnar slowly nodded his head yes. "That man was your biological father and he used to beat me."

"I knew he was my biological father, but I never knew he beat you," said Gunnar.

"He did. He was killed in a bar fight four years ago by a man with a knife. He was a big man, who picked on the wrong guy that night. Coy saw us get left by him and offered us a place to stay until I decided what to do. You and I slept in the same bed down the hall with the chair pressed up under the doorknob for the first two months.

I thought that maybe Coy was a serial killer or something because he was just so nice." Gunnar smiled but didn't laugh. "It's important to me that you know we never slept together until the night he asked me to marry him."

Gunnar nodded his head again that he understood.

"Now for some stuff about the future," she said. "All men are attracted to pretty women with winking eyes and red lips. Don't get hooked up with that. When the makeup and new is worn off, you are left with what was under all of it and it usually isn't much.

Try to find good solid people and keep their friendship. It will be them that stand by you, during the hard times. There will be times you will fail. If you let it, failure can destroy you, but if you learn from it, it will make you stronger. Lastly and most importantly find and marry your best friend. There can be no better thing happen to you than after several years of marriage to realize your spouse is the best friend you have ever had, that's what happened to me.

"I am going to leave you a letter about this and some other things I want you to open on your eighteenth birthday." Gunnar looked down at the floor. He was crying. "It is natural for you to be sad and that's okay but don't feel sorry for me. You have been such a joy in my life. You were my little boy and now you are a young man. I am so proud of what you have become. I've enjoyed more love with you and Coy than most women ever know. Now you better go help your father."

He hugged her for a long time before he went outside, and this time Judith cried.

The next morning Coy was talking about hauling the round bales in and putting the best ones in the barn. Judith asked him if Gunnar could get started on that and if Coy could drive her up into the BLM ground behind the ranch in her buggy.

"Absolutely," said Coy, "but let's let it get good and warm first."

"Maybe we could pack a lunch," she said.

"Now you're talking, I'll start right now," he said going into the kitchen. It was eleven o' clock when they left and Coy took his time and drove slow making sure he didn't bounce her around. He opened the gate at the top, drove through and closed it.

"Let's go to the highest place we can drive to," she said.

Coy looked and started up the incline going west.

When the buggy lost traction he said, "Well, I guess we're here."

She looked all around and said, "Let's go back to that level spot down the hill just a bit."

Coy carefully and slowly backed the side by side down to the spot she had picked. She got out and said, "This is great, we can see the whole valley from here."

They put the blanket down and he brought out the food. He was pouring coffee out of the thermos when he realized she was watching him.

"Thank you Coy," she said. "Thank you for giving me life here on this ranch." He put the thermos down and listened. "Thank you for raising Gunnar. Thank you for loving me as I am. You took us in and brought us to life down there. Gunnar and I became part of that, thank you."

Coy was doing his best to hold it together.

"I know you're going to be sad and grieve when I'm gone but only grieve for yourself. Don't feel sorry for me. I don't even want to think what my life, our life would have been if you hadn't taken us in. My real life started the day you brought us home. Now for the hard part," she said. "It's not natural for a man not even forty years old to live alone."

He raised his head up quickly.

"A man needs a woman by his side, in his house, and in his bed."

Coy started shaking his head no. She reached over and put her hand on his.

"I know this is hard, but if our roles were reversed, you would be telling me this. You don't have to tell me you will find someone, but I want you to look at me and tell me that you understand my wish that you remarry."

Looking down he slowly shook his head.

"Coy Danewood," she said sternly, "You look at me now." Tears were running down his face when he looked up. "If you can't say it," she said, starting to cry herself, "At least nod your head that you understand my wishes."

Coy slowly nodded his head.

Then they hugged each other and cried. He finally stopped crying and she laid down on the blanket and fell asleep. Maybe it was all the stress and strain, but the warm sun felt so good that Coy finally drifted off himself.

A fly landed on his face and woke him. He raised up quickly and looked over to Judith. She was laying with her eyes open. Her tenderness softened Coy and he asked, "Are you hungry now?"

"A little," she said slowly sitting up. They ate their lunch and he pointed out different landmarks that could be seen. They were on their way down when she said, "I want you to remember our talk today." He didn't say anything for a minute or so.

Then he cleared his throat and said, "Judith, I don't think I will ever forget today."

That satisfied her and she reached for and held his hand.

It rained the next day and the men couldn't move the hay, so Judith suggested that Coy bring out the old brown picture album and show Gunnar some of Coy's family history. Judith asked Coy to tell Gunnar about Billy.

Coy thought about where to start. "As I was growing up there were two men my dad's age that seemed to come around often. They were kind of like uncles to me. One was Spider Johnson and the other was Billy Jones. When I was about your age, Billy taught me how to ride in rodeos. When my parents were killed, he took on the job of raising me. When he died suddenly, he left me his ranch and even before that helped me paying off the loan on this place."

"He was rough, loud, and kind of a showoff, but he was my best friend. That is why he is buried here by my mother and father. Have you ever seen the tape we have of him?" he asked.

"Yes," said Gunnar, "but I never knew much about him."

Then they played cards until Judith got tired and went over and laid down on the couch at two in the afternoon. The next day she told Coy to go into town and get her pain medication refilled. He didn't think about it until the lady whispered something to the pharmacist who then brought out the bottle of pain killers to him.

"We are refilling this prescription in a much shorter time than your last refill. Is Mrs. Danewood the only person taking this prescription?"

It hit Coy hard.

"Yes," he said, "she has cancer and there is nothing the doctors can do for her, so I guess she is taking the pills more often. I hadn't noticed it."

"I'm sorry," said the pharmacist, "I had to ask."

Coy paid for the pain medication and slowly drove home.

He found Gunnar moving some of the lower quality hay onto the flat area south of the barn where they stacked it. He motioned for Gunnar to turn off the ignition of the tractor. When he did, he told him about what happened at the pharmacy. He finished by saying, "She will be sleeping a lot more now." Coy could see that his son knew the end was getting closer.

A truck pulled into the yard. Coy didn't know who it was until Spider stepped out. They met on the ground just in front of the front porch.

"I just heard," said Spider, "I am so sorry."

"She is getting weaker now, but I know she'll want to see you," said Coy. He went in the house and left Gunnar out there with Spider.

"How are you doing, son?" Spider asked.

"I guess as good as any boy watching his mother slowly get weaker, it's tough."

"It has to be rough on you," said Spider.

Coy came back out with a more pleasant look on his face. "She's putting on makeup. She wants to look her best when she sees you."

Spider took it okay, but Coy could see his jaw muscles bulging. Coy waited a few minutes and took Spider into the house. Judith held out her hand and he took it.

"Thank you for coming," she said. "Coy please have Gunnar come inside."

As Coy left, Spider said, "I'm so sorry for not coming sooner, I just heard that you were ill."

"I'm just glad you are here now," she said. Then Coy and Gunnar came in. "Gunnar," she said, "I told you to have people of substance for friends. Spider is a person like that. This is what I meant, he has gravel in him and won't let you down when things get rough. You can always count on him. Spider, I want to tell you I love you like an uncle." The tall rangy cowboy dropped his head. "And I know you love me too. Now I have a request."

"Anything," said Spider wiping the tears away with his hand.

"These two men are going to need help when I'm gone. They are going to need a strong person to talk to. I want it to be you."

"Absolutely," said Spider, "you can count on me."

"Thank you, now I'm afraid I'm tired and need to go to sleep. Come over here and give me a kiss," she said. He came over and kissed her gently on her cheek. She didn't cry when she said, "Goodbye."

Spider could feel his tears coming, so he said goodbye and walked to the front door.

Outside he looked away from the house and took out his handkerchief to wipe his eyes. He turned back to Coy and Gunnar. "I hope you two never forget how special she is." Then he walked to his truck slowly shaking his head and drove away.

Judith only lasted two weeks after Spider came to see her. The day after he left, she gave Gunnar his letter to open on his eighteenth birthday and Coy one to open on Thanksgiving Day. In her last conscious moment, she told each of them how much she loved them, then she was gone.

To Coy it was an effort just to breathe. He could hear Gunnar softly crying beside him and knew he should say something, but he wasn't able to speak.

They sat silently on her bed for almost twenty minutes before Coy found the strength to finally say, "Her suffering is now over."

He could see Gunnar slowly nodding his head yes. Gunnar was finally able to say, "Yes, it is."

Coy then stood up and called the funeral home.

CHAPTER 11

The Funeral

They stood on the front porch together, Coy's arm around Gunnar's shoulder as the ambulance took Judith into town. Spider drove to the house about two hours later. He told Coy he was there to help them get through it and asked if they wanted to go make arrangements then or wait until tomorrow. Coy said they should go ahead and do it then. Spider drove them into town and the men made all the arrangements for Judith's funeral.

News travels fast in a small town. Jesse heard about Judith's passing and told her mom and grandfather that night at the dinner table. Darlene never cared for the woman, but the news still seemed to sadden her. Adam

McDaniels never said a word. Later that night when Spider couldn't sleep, he thought he would go up and ask for some time off. After hearing his boss's words on the phone he turned and left.

Food started arriving earlier that night at the Danewood Ranch. The neighboring ranchers' wives got together and decided to take turns taking food out to Coy and Gunnar. The next night Jean and Phil drove out. She brought fried chicken, mashed potatoes and some gravy Coy had bragged so much about. He showed her all the food he already had in the refrigerator and asked what he could do with it.

"Freeze it," she said. "Freeze it and eat it later," she added nodding her head. She grabbed Coy by both arms and looked up at him. "Are you guys going to be all right?"

"I guess," he said. "This time it's different, we knew this day would come."

"If you bottom out sometime and need to talk, you call me," she said. He nodded his head slowly that he understood. She did not let him go. "I mean it," she said, "if you get down or blue you call me!"

He finally smiled a little when he said, "Okay Jean, I'll call you."

"That's better," she said trying to be tough, then she and Phil left.

Coy had Gunnar help him and together they froze most of the food. It worked out well because it took them until 10:30 and by then they were tired and slept. The Jenkins drove over the next day at two in the afternoon.

"Did you see the news at noon?" Mr. Jenkins asked.

"No," said Coy, "we haven't watched the news lately."

"Adam McDaniels is dead," said Mr. Jenkins.

Coy thought he had heard it wrong and leaned forward and was instantly serious. "Did you say Adam McDaniels is dead?"

"He was killed in a car accident early this morning. His Cadillac slid off the highway north of Taos, went down a mountain and caught on fire. It took most of the morning to figure out who he was. I guess he was pretty burned up."

"That's Jesse's grandfather," said Gunnar.

"Yes, she and Darlene live at the big house with him," said Mr. Jenkins.

"Do you think I should go see her?" Gunnar ask his father.

"I don't know," said Coy. He thought about it a little and then said, "I guess you could go over and knock on the door. The worst Darlene could do is run you off. If you go, make sure you don't stay long."

"Okay," said Gunnar.

"If it is going fairly well tell her that we, both of us send our condolences."

"Can you believe it?" asked Mr. Jenkins after Gunnar left. "After all the things McDaniels pulled to get more land, now he gets killed in a car wreck."

"I guess in the end it didn't do him much good, did it?" asked Coy.

"No, it didn't," said Mr. Jenkins. "Well, we better go home," he said before walking back to his truck and driving away.

Coy was left by himself so he saddled up his best horse, rode it up to the house and left a note that he was riding the BLM ground behind the house. He hadn't been up there since he and Judith had that picnic. He wanted to go up there and remember their day together.

Over at the McDaniels Ranch, Gunnar knocked softly on the door. When no one answered, he rang the doorbell. Jesse slowly opened the door. When she saw who it was, she was instantly outside hugging him and crying. She was crying and trying to speak but it all ran together. Gunnar rocked her and patted her on her back. He could feel her begin to relax and start pulling it together. He reached back and found his handkerchief and gave it to her. She wiped her eyes and blew her nose then took a half step back.

"Thank you for coming," she said. Darlene came to the door with red eyes and a flushed face.

"We just wanted to come and give our condolences," he said softly.

"Thank you," said Darlene, "Don't be too long Jesse." She closed the door.

The kids just stood there. Finally, Gunnar asked, "Is there anything I can do for you?"

"Thanks for asking but I don't guess there is anything anyone can do. My grandpa is dead, and he is gone forever. I still can't hardly believe it."

"Accidents like this come out of the blue, no one is ever ready for this to happen. If you need to talk just call. We can meet or I'll come here."

She smiled a little for the first time.

"Well I guess I'll go back home then," said Gunnar.

She came forward pulled him down and kissed him on the side of his face and said, "Thank you." He held her for a moment then turned and left.

Two men drove up to the Danewood Ranch the next day in a full-size, four-door sedan. Coy looked at the pair in suits and thought they might have something to do with the utility company. They introduced themselves as detectives for the Highway Patrol. Gunnar walked up as the men each showed Coy their badges. The shorter of the two appeared to be in charge and asked if Coy was acquainted with Adam McDaniels. Coy said that he was.

Then the other man asked, "When was the last time you saw him?"

"Man, let me think," said Coy, "It's been a while. I can't remember seeing him for years."

"And his daughter, how long has it been since you have seen her?" snapped the shorter one.

"A couple of months ago. Now why are you asking me all these questions?" asked Coy.

"Did you have a grudge against Adam McDaniels?" The taller detective asked.

"I'm not going to stand here and be raked over the coals by you unless you tell me what's up."

"Where were you two nights ago on Monday evening?" asked the shorter one. Both detectives caught the change in Coy.

Quietly he said, "Monday night I was here at the house. My wife had died that morning and I was here at home. We both were," he said pointing over to Gunnar.

"Can you prove that?" snapped the shorter detective.

"That does it, I'm going to ask you two to leave now."

"And if we don't?" asked the same detective.

"You don't want to go there."

"We understand you are a violent man Mr. Danewood."

"I want to talk to my lawyer before you grill me anymore. Now you two get off my property."

The taller of the two kind of pulled at the shorter one's arm. "Let's go and come back with a warrant," he said. That made the shorter one smile. "We'll be back," he said before walking over to their car. Coy didn't like that look on the face of the one detective just before they left.

"I think I better call John Hull up in Trinity," said Coy.

"I think you better," said his son. "They think you had something to do with Adam McDaniels' death."

Coy came back outside after making his phone call. John told him not to answer any more questions and that it should take them at least another day to get a warrant, if they could get one. He didn't feel they would be able to. If they came back, John said to tell them that Coy would gladly show up at the local police station with his attorney, but he would need a couple of days to prepare.

John also said that just as soon as Coy hung up the phone that he and Gunnar should write down where they were and everyone they saw and at what time for the last two days, just in case.

The detectives drove up to the McDaniels Ranch. They told Darlene that her father's death was not an accident. She tried to get them to tell her why they thought that, but they wouldn't say. Then they asked her how she got along with her father. Spider had followed the men into the big house.

"Why are you asking her that?" he asked.

"We ask the questions here. Did your father have a large life insurance policy?" the taller man asked.

"I think you guys need to leave," said Spider. "Darlene will have a lawyer present the next time you talk to her. You two are worse than useless. I'll bet you haven't even checked out the man himself. Adam McDaniels was very successful and had lots of enemies. To accomplish what he did he had to deal with some bad people."

"You seem to know an awful lot Mr. Johnson, where were you the night before the accident?"

"Here at the ranch, I always sleep here."

"Can you prove that?"

"I don't have to, I've already told you, now it's time for you guys to leave."

After the men left ,Spider told Darlene to call the family attorney. "You have enough to take care of right now without those two idiots making your life hard."

John Hull called Coy the next morning. Coy and Gunnar were out but they listened to the message twice on the answering machine. John said he asked around and found that McDaniels' Cadillac had been tampered with and there were rumors around that the police had a video of someone doing something to it in a hotel parking lot in Taos the night before the accident. John closed by saying to call him back and they would talk about Coy's and Gunnar's notes about the last two days. Coy called him back and together all three talked about what they had written about their whereabouts.

Spider went over to the Danewood Ranch that afternoon. He said he stopped by to see how they were doing. The conversation turned to McDaniels' accident and Coy told him what John Hull had said.

"It doesn't surprise me," said Spider. "Remember that time I showed you that clipping about the college professor getting beat up?"

"Yes," said Coy.

"Adam dealt with people like that."

"I remember Billy telling me up in Denver that McDaniels hired thugs up there to work me over," said Coy. "He said you told him."

"That's true, but I think we might better forget about that, because that would give you a reason to get even."

"I see what you mean," said Coy, "I seem to have forgotten all about that just now."

Spider laughed. "Listen I'm going to be pretty busy with Darlene and little Jesse for a while and might not see you until Judith's service, but I guarantee you I'll be there. Okay?"

"We understand," said Coy.

After Spider drove away, Coy looked over to his son and asked, "Did you hear him refer to Jesse as Little Jesse?"

"Yes."

"Billy said he took care of Darlene just like she was his own daughter. I guess he thinks of Jesse as still a little girl. Kind of nice isn't it?"

Gunnar was watching Spider's pickup drive away when he said, "Yes, it is."

Coy drove them to town and bought new white shirts and a sport coat for Gunnar. When he looked at his son in the mirror at the store, he realized that Gunnar was now taller than him. Then he drove over to the funeral home and asked about Judith's wedding rings.

In the truck he handed the little box to Gunnar and said, "We are going to open a safety deposit box now and put all your mother's jewelry in it. She told me she wanted you to have it. That way if anything happens to me, you can go get it. Tomorrow you bring the rest of it and put it in the safety deposit box."

They went to the bank and set it up with

both names on the signature card so either he or Gunnar could go in at any time and open the box.

Jesse found the obituary for Judith in the newspaper and found the day and the time of the funeral. It was three days before her grandfather's funeral, and she knew she couldn't ask her mother, so she made her plans to attend the graveside service on her own. She drove into town and bought a black blouse and black jacket.

The day of the funeral Coy felt a weight bearing down on him. He didn't say anything to Gunnar about it, but his son could see the difference in his father. Coy changed from his Levi's into a pair of slacks, then put on the long sleeve white shirt and tried to tie his tie. Gunnar heard him say something about a blamed tie and went into his dad's room. The first thing he noticed was that Coy's forehead was shiny with sweat. It wasn't warm in the house.

"I'll help you Dad," he said taking over tying the tie.

"Today is getting to me," Coy said.

"I know, let's just give Mom a nice service okay?"

"Yeah, let's just give her a real nice service." He still didn't look at Gunnar.

It had rained earlier that day but had stopped and turned into a clear beautiful day. They were sitting on the front porch when the hearse drove up. Coy saw Gunnar drop his head. The hearse moved slowly up the side of the yard followed by several vehicles. Coy and Gunnar walked up to the family plot and sat in the chairs that had been put there for them. Spider was in the third truck. He parked and walked up to Coy and Gunnar.

Coy looked at his old friend and said, "You better stay close. I'm probably going to need you today."

"You bet," said Spider.

The cars had all but stopped driving in by 10:55. Judith would have been surprised at how many people showed up. Ranchers and their wives drove in from miles around knowing who Coy was. She had always loved yellow roses. Coy had ordered a spray of four dozen to be placed on the casket. He watched them place it on the casket almost covering it.

Right at eleven o'clock a lady from the local church started singing a song that had four verses. Everyone was standing and no one saw Jesse McDaniels ride her horse up, tie him down by the cars and walk up. She moved along the edge of the people and slowly walked up behind Gunnar and slipped her hand into his. She was surprised when he nodded his head that she was there before even looking over to her. His eyes were shiny with tears.

Up on the ridge overlooking the valley below, Darlene McDaniels was watching the service from her spot where she had always watched what happened down at Coy's ranch. She saw Jesse take Gunnar's hand and felt her eyes fill with tears. She studied Coy closely. His clothes just hung on him, it looked like he had lost thirty pounds.

Just before the preacher finished, Coy had to sit down. He had almost collapsed. She could see him crying hard. Spider was there trying to console him. She lowered her head and began to cry. She knew at that moment she had to go to him.

There were only four people left in line to give their condolences when Darlene walked up. Spider came over and put his hand firmly on her forearm. She looked up at him with red eyes and said, "Don't worry, I'm only here to say how sorry I am for both of them." Spider nodded his head and stood beside her.

Jesse was shocked to see her mother when she stepped forward. Darlene reached out and put her hand on Gunnar's face. "I am so sorry for your loss," she said.

"Thank you," said Gunnar, looking at her through his own tears.

Darlene moved over to Coy. He started to stand. Darlene reached out and put her hand on his shoulder. "Don't, please don't," she said, "I'm only here to say how sorry I am for your loss. It is so evident how much you loved her."

Coy didn't talk, he couldn't talk, he just nodded his head.

Darlene made a small movement with her hand to have Spider come over to her. "Will you make sure Jesse gets safely home?"

"Sure, I'll do that," he said.

She thanked him and slowly walked away. She was reaching for her door handle when she heard it. Someone was yelling, "No! No! No!"

She turned and saw Coy clinging to the casket before the men started to lower it into the ground. She turned back around to her truck leaned her forehead against it and just stood there and cried.

Up on the hill Spider finally convinced Coy that he had to walk away and let the men lower the casket into the grave. He, Coy and Gunnar slowly walked down to the house. Once inside, Spider asked if they had coffee. Coy didn't speak but Gunnar took him into the kitchen and showed him the coffee maker.

Spider tasted the coffee, made a face and said, "That's awful. We'll make some more." He poured out the lukewarm stuff and after Gunnar showed him where the coffee and filters were, he made a fresh pot of strong coffee.

He walked around the living room and spotted Coy's belt buckles. "I want to tell you something Gunnar," he said. "When your dad threw a rope at a calf, it just didn't miss. I know, I've roped against him. He wasn't always the fastest, but he just never missed. If he ever had a good run the rest of us were just trying to get second place. Now we had better talk about cattle before I leave. Coy have you listened to the markets lately?"

Coy didn't speak he just shook his head no.

"Well I have, and it looks like the feedlots are a little hungry. Gunnar, you help your dad watch the markets and numbers of calves being sold. You don't want to be last in line to sell your calves this year. Fact is with everything that has happened I think I would sell early. We are at the McDaniels Ranch," he said. "Speaking of the ranch, I have to get back to it. Are you two going to be okay here?"

Gunnar said yes, but Coy barely nodded his head.

Spider motioned for Gunnar to follow him outside. On the porch he said, "Don't push him hard today, but tomorrow get him outside and up in the BLM ground on a horse. I know that man, he'll come around if you can get him outside and on a horse."

Gunnar thanked him and said goodbye.

Spider pulled up behind the big house at the ranch and sat in his truck for a bit. He found Darlene sitting on the couch softly crying. She stood, walked up and hugged him and continued to cry.

They talked until Jesse came in. She caught it right off, there was a difference in her mother. Jesse couldn't figure out what it was and then it came to her. Somehow her mother seemed older or softer somehow, for sure she was not as tough or stern as she used to be.

CHAPTER 12

Two Men Were Arrested

It was all over the local television station and newspaper the next morning. The state detectives said that two men were arrested in connection with Adam McDaniels' death. They had a video of them buying gas that night in Taos and they had a separate video of one of them tampering with the Cadillac. Phone records proved a long association between them and Adam McDaniels. The news anchor ended the story by saying both men had long rap sheets for violent behavior.

Gunnar did what Spider suggested and got Coy on a horse and up into the BLM. They jumped a big buck deer with a large set of horns.

"Boy," said Coy, "he's a big one."

Gunnar looked over at him with a little smile and said, "He sure is."

That seemed to break the spell. They rode and talked about the ranch and cattle and how much hay they had. Gunnar made it last as long as he could.

He was closing the gate behind the house when Coy asked, "How did we ever get so lucky to live here? I mean look around, there are mountains on the sides and the valley down below where we live. A nice creek running beside the highway down there. How did you and I get lucky enough to ever live here?"

"I hear you Dad, I guess I've grown up here and take it for granted. We do live in a beautiful place." Gunnar put up the horses then came into the house and found his dad watching the cattle market reports on television.

It was only nine days until school started and Gunnar wanted to ride about every second day. They were putting up the horses after the third ride when Coy told him, "We're liable to wear these horses out with you getting me out of the house and up on a horse like this." Gunnar slowly turned and looked to his Dad.

"I'm not all the way back, but I'm doing pretty good," he said. "You don't have to babysit me anymore. Besides school starts next week, so you better get into town and buy some new clothes." Gunnar then turned back and continued working on the horses.

Gunnar's classmates were proud to be

seniors. Jesse took drama and learned just before lunch that she got the part of the grieving widow in the upcoming school play. She thought she would go tell Gunnar. She found him sitting in a group of kids, Beth on one side and Susan James on the other. Susan was sitting too close. She let it go and decided to tell him later.

The next morning, she drove her pickup into the front yard of the Danewood Ranch. Both men came out to see who it was. She walked up and hugged Coy tightly.

"How are you doing?" she asked pulling back.

"Much better after that hug," he said smiling at her.

"I need to chew on your son for a minute."

"Okay," said Coy, "I'll go back in the house and let you kids have the front porch."

Gunnar moved his left arm in a sweeping motion towards the porch meaning after you. She climbed the steps and started in as he came up.

"How come you never come to school functions?"

"I don't know."

"You never come to football games."

"No."

"And you never come to basketball games."

"No," he said then added, "but I'll bet Bill does."

"What about dances?"

"Nope."

She just stood there and looked at him. "Are

you afraid?"

"Of what?"

"Dances."

"Maybe, I don't know."

"Well, can you dance?"

"I don't know I've never tried."

"You need to go to some of these events."

"How come?"

"Because that's what kids do. Look, it's our senior year and if you don't come to some of these things, you'll regret it. I have a leading role in the school play. I'm the grieving widow. Are you going to come and see me?"

"When is it?"

"November twentieth, just before we let out for Thanksgiving."

"I'll have to check to see if I have a date that night," he said. She stepped forward and pushed him with both hands in his chest. He almost fell off the front porch.

"Okay, okay," he said laughing, "I just checked my calendar and I don't have a date that night."

"Will you come for sure?"

"I'll be there."

"Okay we'll work on dancing later then."

"I didn't agree to that," he said.

She paused for a second and said, "That really doesn't matter." Then she hopped down the steps to her truck and drove away.

Two weeks later at lunch, Susan James the girl that sat next to him before, came up and sat down next to him in the cafeteria. She was a junior and ran barrels in all the local youth rodeos.

"What's new with you Gunnar?" she asked.

"Not much, how about you?"

"I'm looking for someone to take me to the school play on the twentieth."

"Are you asking me to take you?"

"Yes, if you will, no if you won't," she said and smiled.

He had to laugh. There was talk around that Susan was a little wild.

"How could I turn that down, I guess it's a yes," he said.

"Great," she said, leaning forward smiling.

Jesse drove straight over to the Danewood Ranch after school the next day. She was standing there leaning against her truck when Gunnar drove in. He was concerned and got out quickly.

"Is anything the matter?" he asked.

"Maybe, what's the deal with Susan James?"

Gunnar was surprised and leaned away from her. She came forward and asked, "Are you guys dating?"

"No, she asked me to take her to the school play and since you wanted me there, I said I'd take her."

"Oh," Jesse said relieved.

"Are you jealous?"

"Maybe a little," she said. "Tell your dad if he had been here, I would've kissed him." Then she burst out laughing and drove home. Gunnar was smiling watching her drive out the drive.

The school play was well received and

finished without a problem. The audience brought them out a second time for more applause. Gunnar never saw anything like it. It was easy to see that Jesse was the best and brightest of the students in the cast.

The members came down afterwards to talk to their parents in the crowd. Jesse was talking to her mother and Spider when the crowd thinned out and in one short opening, she saw Gunnar. He gave her a thumbs up, then Susan leaned in from the side and waved to Jesse. She was still in costume of an old widow when she walked up to them.

"You look good tonight," said Gunnar right off, "But you seem a little older." Then he laughed.

Jesse smiled and asked, "Are you guys going to stay for the party tonight?"

"We can't, we have other plans," said Susan opening her eyes wide open.

"Oh, I see," said Jesse before giving Gunnar a look and walking away. She changed her clothes and went to the party. Brad, the boy that had played opposite of her in the play, stayed by her all night and offered her a ride home, but she declined.

Coy and Gunnar were in the town cafe one week after the school play. Spider Johnson came in and they waved him over. As soon as Spider sat down, he looked at Coy and asked, "You ever see an ostrich pick cotton?"

Coy winked at Gunnar and said, "Nope, I never have."

"Me neither," said Spider smiling.

Several of the customers close enough laughed. The waitress had already brought Coy and Gunnar water, but she didn't bother with Spider. She brought his usual cup of strong black coffee.

Spider told her that lunch was on him and give these two knot heads anything they wanted. They were sitting there making small talk when they saw the man come in. He asked the waitress a question and she pointed over to the table where Spider and the Danewoods were sitting. He walked up and asked which one was Mr. Johnson. When Spider said that was him the man introduced himself as Jack Martin and said he was the attorney representing the two men charged with Adam McDaniels' murder.

He asked if he could speak to Mr. Johnson alone outside. Spider said yes, got up and followed the man outside. Coy didn't like the look of it and told Gunnar to stay where he was, he was going out there.

The attorney had already started when Coy walked up but stopped when he saw him stand next to Spider. Coy looked at Spider and nodded his head one time and his older friend nodded back to him.

Turning back to the attorney Spider said, "It's okay, anything you have to say to me you can say in front of Coy here."

The attorney started again. He said he looked at the state's evidence and found that the video of his two clients in the convenience store was taken within three minutes of the video the state had of the hotel parking lot. The convenience store was on the other side of town from the hotel parking lot. There was no way the two men could have driven over and tampered with the Cadillac. The attorney looked from side to side to make sure no one else could hear and said that his clients told him that Adam and themselves were the only ones that knew he was going to be in Taos that night, so someone had to follow Adam McDaniels from the ranch to mess with the car.

"Why are you telling us this?" asked Spider.

"I thought before all this came out and the police put two and two together, the McDaniels Ranch might wish to pay for my clients defense." Then the man smiled in a way that neither Coy, nor Spider liked.

"I pity your poor clients," said Coy. The man lost his smile. "You can't be very bright coming into town and asking the ranch to pay for the defense of the two men that sabotaged Adam McDaniels' car. You need to get out of town before you're thrown out."

"Is that a threat?" asked the crooked attorney with an evil smile.

Coy started forward but Spider put his hand on his chest stopping him and said, "Leave right now."

"You've made a big mistake today," said the attorney before walking over to his car.

"I doubt that very much," said Coy.

The two friends stood together in the parking lot and watched the attorney drive away. Spider looked around to make sure no one could hear them, then asked, "Is there anything you want to ask me Coy?

"Nothing I can think of."

"Okay," said Spider, "Then let's go eat."

Gunnar never knew what was said outside he just noticed how serious both men were when they came back in and didn't talk and joke like always as they ate their meal. The two men never talked about that conversation again.

CHAPTER 13

Sorry For Everything

Thanksgiving Day Coy got up early and went into the kitchen. He made coffee and opened the letter Judith left for him.

Coy,

I'm so glad you have made it this far and I know a lot of what people see is just a front that you put on. It is time to get on with your life. I want you to go out today and say goodbye to me at my grave. I am gone. I know you don't want to hear it, but you are too young to live the rest of your life alone. I know you remember our talk of you finding someone and remarrying. It is time. Now go out to my grave and say goodbye.

Love,
Judith

Coy felt outside himself. He cried softly. Even in death she knew him so well. He faked it most of the time. Judith was gone and he knew it, he had to accept it. It was time to say goodbye. It was a slow and hard climb walking up to the grave.

"Oh Judith," he said, "I miss you. Yes, I have been faking it and it is getting very tiring. I think you are right, it is time to start living again. Thank you for everything, for our lives together, for allowing me to make Gunnar my son. I owe you so much. I know if you were here, you would say it was the other way around, but it's not, it's just not. Thank you for every bit of it and now I have to say goodbye to you. Goodbye Judith." He slowly turned and walked away.

He thought about it and decided to let Gunnar read the letter his mother had left for him. When he finished, Gunnar looked up.

"She is right," said Coy, "I have been faking it. It's time to quit faking and start being real again."

"Can I help?" asked Gunnar.

"I don't think so, I have to find my own way. You need to know I will probably get quiet and blue sometimes."

Gunnar nodded his understanding.

Darlene drove her shiny pickup into the

front yard of the Danewood Ranch six days before Christmas and just sat in her truck. Coy waited and when she didn't get out, he finally walked out to her. To him she looked kind of scared.

"Darlene?" he asked.

She started to speak then stopped. She tried again the second time and got the words out. "I was wondering if I could put flowers on Judith's grave?"

He was shocked, they hadn't liked each other. She appeared to be trying to do the right thing.

"That would be fine," he said.

"Would you go with me?" she asked timidly.

"Yes, I'll go with you."

She laid the fresh cut flowers on the ground in front of Judith's headstone.

"I have been talking to the preacher here in town," she said. "He has been helping me understand a lot of things." Then she hung her head and began to cry softly. "The preacher says to go to people you have wronged and ask forgiveness, but I'm too late for Judith. I want you to know, I am truly sorry for everything I have done and said to you and her. Can you ever forgive me?"

"If it wasn't for second chances where would any of us be, of course I forgive you Darlene."

"So much has happened, you lost Judith, I lost my dad, then found out he was murdered. Then I received this letter from a woman claiming to be my mother," she said handing the letter to him. He opened the letter and saw the multiple pages. It was mid-December and a cold wind was blowing.

"Would you feel comfortable going into the house? It's pretty cold out here."

She nodded her head then looking over to the headstone said, "I am so sorry Judith, you didn't deserve it."

They went down to the house and went inside. Darlene was shocked.

"I've never been in here since you remodeled. I always thought it would be rough, kind of like a bunkhouse."

Coy smiled and said, "Please have a seat," He gestured to a chair at the large dining room table. He read each of the five pages then looked up at her. "Wait right here," he said before walking down the hall. "Ah," he said, and came back with a picture. "Does that look like anyone you know?" he asked, handing it to her.

Darlene was shocked. She looked at the picture then looked up at Coy then back down to the picture.

"Is this her?"

"Yes."

"Where did you get this?"

"Billy Jones. When they were young, he fell in love with your mother. He even helped her leave the night she left. He kept it on his mantel."

"I can't believe it. She's alive? I always thought she died."

"She didn't. My mother told me about it when I was a teenager. She said your mother came to her and said that she was going to leave. Your father had beaten and broken her down mentally until she had nothing left. If she took you, your father would find her and bring her back. She told my mother she feared for her life if that happened. My mother told me several people in town helped her and Billy told me Spider brought her to him, then he took her to the bus station. Now think back, remember him staring at you when we were kids."

"Yes! I remember that."

"It sounds like she would really like to see you."

"Oh Coy." She laid her head on her arms and cried on the table just sitting there. He got up, went into the kitchen and got a kitchen towel for her to wipe her eyes.

"I have made such a mess of my life. I have been filled with anger and hatred for most of it. I hated Judith and the only reason was because she had you. That's all she ever did. I never gave her a chance. I have held anger in my heart for my mother for not being in my life and now I find out she was abused by my father. I have made such a mess of my life."

He stood there and let her get it all out. She finally realized that he had quit talking and began to dry her face with the towel and said, "I should probably go."

"Please don't go just yet. I have something to say. Judith wrote me a letter to open after she passed. I read it just a few weeks ago. She said that probably I have been putting on a front and, well I have. I'm going to do my best to be real from now on and like right now," he said wiping his tears on his shirtsleeve. "If I cry, I cry, but I'm done faking it and I think that maybe it's time for you to be real too."

She nodded her head that she understood. "You have always been so nice."

He smiled and said, "Not always."

"Well maybe not once," she said and laughed lightly.

"I have always been ashamed of that."

"Don't be," she said, quickly putting her hand on his. He looked down on her hand and she pulled it back.

"Gunnar and I go to church on Sundays, why don't you come next week?" he asked.

She said she would think about it, thanked him for everything and left holding her mother's picture that Coy had given her.

She called Coy and asked if he would meet her at the town cafe for coffee two weeks later. He said he would, got cleaned up and drove into town. She waved him over to her booth with a happy smile. She thanked him for coming and was happy about something.

"I called my mother and she asked to come here, see me, and meet Jesse. We talked for almost an hour. I told her of you and your parents, and she remembered them. She will be here in two days, would you like to meet her?"

"I would, there is so much to tell her, like my folks, Billy, just all kinds of stuff. Where and when?" he asked.

"We are going to meet here then go somewhere else. She doesn't want to go out to our ranch because of bad memories." Darlene paused and seemed to be searching for words.

"Would you like to have everyone come out to my place?"

"I really would, if it wouldn't be too much of a problem."

"It won't be a problem at all. I would love to show her Mom and Dad and Billy's graves and tell her he loved her all his life."

She put her hand on his and said, "Thank you Coy, this means a lot to me."

He made no effort to move his hand that time. They just sat there looking at each other until the waitress brought their coffee. Only then did he pull his hand back.

Gunnar came home from school and found his dad cleaning the house. Coy told him everything quickly as he was sweeping out the hall and started in on the kitchen. Gunnar changed his clothes and helped his dad.

They dusted everything and mopped the floors last thing before they went to bed. Gunnar went to school the next day and Coy put the finishing touches on the house. That evening Coy called Darlene and together they set up a time for everyone to meet at the cafe, then come out to the Danewood Ranch.

Spider, Jesse and Darlene were standing inside the cafe when Gunnar and Coy walked in. Everyone said hello, then Spider said, "Let's grab a couple of tables and pull them together."

Gunnar came over to Jesse and told her how nice she looked. She thanked him politely and said that it looked like he could have brushed a little more dirt off his pants. He looked down quickly and she started laughing, then went over, grabbed Coy by the arm and pulled him down and kissed him on his cheek.

"It's good to see you," she said.

He stopped walking and looked over to Gunnar and said, "You better watch out for me."

Everyone laughed. He motioned for Jesse to sit next to her mother then went over and sat down between Darlene and Spider. Jesse saw where he sat and raised her eyebrows at Gunnar twice.

"I'm so nervous," said Darlene. "What if we don't recognize her?"

"We'll know her, she will look just like you only twenty-five years older," said Spider.

The door opened and a woman walked in and Spider's mouth hung open. The woman saw him, then looked over to Darlene and smiled. She walked over to them.

Spider stood and held out his arms. "Sarah," he said, "my God, it is really you."

She put her hand on his face and said "Yes, Spider, it's me." She looked around him and saw Darlene who was walking toward her. "Now let me go and let me hug my daughter," she said.

Tears were running down both women's faces as they hugged each other. Coy took out his own handkerchief and wiped his tears away. Gunnar appeared to be the only one not crying, so he gave Jesse his handkerchief.

When Sarah could talk, she told Darlene, "I

never thought I would get a chance to hold you again."

Coy had stood hearing her, came over and said, "Sarah I am..." He never got to finish because she cut him off.

"Your Tom Danewood's son." Coy was taken aback. "Is this your son?"

"Yes.""

Then the woman's eyes went over to Jesse. "Darlene is this lovely girl my granddaughter?" Jesse stood and started to walk around.

"Yes, this is my daughter, Jesse Marie McDaniels."

Sarah looked at Darlene for a moment after hearing the last name then back over to Jesse. She left one arm around Darlene and said, "Come on, I'm going to go hug your daughter." They took a few steps together and Sarah hugged Jesse with one arm, still hugging Darlene with the other. "What a day," she said looking up to the ceiling and saying, "Thank you Father, for allowing me to finally hold these two girls."

"Should we all go out to my place so we can sit around and talk?" Coy asked.

Everyone looked to Sarah.

"I don't care," she said, "As long as I can hang on to these two."

Everyone was still laughing as they went outside and divided up into the four-door pickups ,then drove over to the Danewood Ranch.

Sarah was shocked walking up the front steps. "I don't remember this house being this big."

"We remodeled it," said Coy opening the door for her.

Inside she said, "Your house is beautiful." Coy built a big fire in the fireplace and as he looked around, he thought yes, the house did look good.

They sat around the table and talked the entire morning. Coy stood and motioned for Gunnar to follow him into the kitchen.

"We have to feed these people," he whispered.

"Okay," said Gunnar. He went over and opened the refrigerator.

"Coy!" called out Sarah.

"Yes ma'am," he said.

"What are you two doing in there?"

"Well we're trying to rustle up a little food for everyone."

"No, you're not," she said standing. "Come on ladies, have you forgot I was born and raised out here in cowboy country?" Then she was in the kitchen and told him "You just show us women where everything is, and we will do the cooking."

After being run out of his own kitchen, Coy sat at the dining room table and answered questions the women had about where the food and utensils were. Later, when the conversation had begun to slow down, Coy took everyone out to the grave sites and showed her Jonesy's grave. It had started snowing very small flakes making the air even look white.

"I know he would have wanted me to tell you

he was sorry he never told you how much he loved you," said Coy. Darlene saw Coy look over to Judith's grave. He stopped smiling and lowered his head.

Sarah had small tears rolling down her face. She reached for Spider's arm and pulled him close. He turned and hugged her. "I never thanked you for your help that night," she said.

"You had a lot on your mind," said Spider, "It's really not important."

"You did what I asked you to do. You have looked after Darlene all these years."

"And still does," added Darlene.

"How can one person's life get so messed up and then come back together and be so wonderful?" asked Sarah.

"Because one man messed it up, that's why," said Spider.

"I have a VCR tape of Billy in the house of us at a rodeo, would you like to see it?" asked Coy.

"Yes, very much," said Darlene's mother.

The visit ended with everyone in the house watching the tape of Billy and Coy at the rodeo. Darlene was sitting next to Coy on the couch with a space between them. She saw him wipe his eyes with his handkerchief and remembering his words about not faking it, reached over and held his hand. He nodded his head just a little. Both kids saw it and looked over at each other. Jesse rolled her eyes.

Darlene then asked her mother if she felt she could stay out at the McDaniels Ranch. She could see her mother struggle trying to find the right words.

"I would rather not, if it doesn't offend you."

"Of course not," said Darlene.

"How about if you stay at my little place behind the big house?" asked Spider. She looked at him surprised that he would ask such a thing.

"I mean I could stay in the big house and you could use my place."

"Better not leave him alone with your mother Darlene," said Coy. Everyone but Spider laughed.

"You're an idiot," he said to Coy.

"That would be fine, I'll stay out at Spider's house," she said.

Everyone went outside to leave, and Darlene turned and hugged Gunnar, then Coy and said, "Thank you for having all of us out here."

"You're more than welcome, we had a really good time here today."

Everyone waved goodbye and their visitors left.

CHAPTER 14

What Have You Two Been Up To

Darlene drove out to the Danewood Ranch while the kids were in school. Coy stepped off the last step of his front porch. She took two quick steps, hugged him hard and kissed him on the side of his face.

"My mother just left," she said. "We had such a good time together. Jesse really got to know her grandmother. It was so, so good. She told me I have a half-sister and a half-brother just south of Tulsa Oklahoma." She finally stopped and realized that she was still holding him. Her face changed from excitement to a warm smile. "Oh," she said, and let him go.

"You didn't leave her alone with Spider, did you?"

"No," she said laughing and hugged him again. Letting him go she said, "I'm sorry I'm just so happy."

"It's really good to see. Want to come in for a minute?"

"Sure," she said grabbing his arm in hers. They walked up the steps together that way. She stayed for almost an hour talking about her mother. Out in the yard, before she left, she took his hands in hers.

"It's been so long since I have cared for anyone. Coy, can I kiss you?"

It took him a minute, but then he said, "Yes."

She came forward and kissed him very politely and softly on his lips. His eyes were open but hers were not.

"You are going to have to watch out for me, Coy Danewood," she said smiling then winked at him and left.

He walked out to Judith's grave.

"I feel so mixed up, Judith. Darlene just kissed me, and it felt soft and nice. You have been the love of my life and that will never change, but other things are happening now. I just want you to know no one will ever take your place in my heart."

That afternoon when Jesse came in, she told her mother, "We need to talk."

Darlene couldn't remember hearing Jesse being that direct before, so she said okay and followed her into the living room.

"I need to know, is Coy Danewood my father?"

Darlene sat down on the sofa and said, "No, absolutely not."

"You haven't ever said much about it and I need to know for sure."

"I guess if your old enough to ask, you're old enough to hear the truth. It's not pretty." She paused trying to find where to start. "I moved down to Albuquerque and started college. I met a professor that seemed so polished and sophisticated. He was so different from people I had grown up with. To make a long story short, I became pregnant with you and he bluntly said he would never marry me. It was at that very moment I saw through all the glamor and saw that he was hollow inside. All he cared about was himself. I came home, had you and here we are. I hope you don't despise me," she said softly.

"Then you and Coy have never slept together?"

"Oh honey, do you have to ask these questions?"

"Judith said something that day at their house, that struck a nerve in Coy. I saw it."

"Yes, she did. Coy and I had a picnic way up high on the mountain where our places join ,just after we graduated. A storm came up and soaked us to the skin. One thing led to another and we made love that one time up there. That was almost fourteen months before you were born. I hope this answers all your questions."

"Just one more," Jesse said sitting down next to her. "Did you ever get over him?"

Her mother took a long time to answer.

"No, I didn't and haven't," she said and looked directly at her.

"Okay Mom," said Jesse. "Now things make a lot more sense to me. I won't say a word unless you say it is okay."

"Thank you honey, I know what I want, but I don't know if I can have it."

"I understand Mom," said Jesse. Then the two hugged each other for a long time.

Snow fell and stayed. Coy and Gunnar were feeding lots of hay and were out with the cattle quite a lot. Maybe that's why they were shocked that Saturday afternoon in early February when a shiny four-wheel drive pickup drove in. They went outside to see who it was.

Jesse stepped out and yelled, "Do you guys have any hot chocolate?" They just stood there and looked at each other. "It doesn't matter," she yelled, "I brought my own."

She reached in and pulled a bag out of the truck and started walking their way. "Here," she said giving the bag to Gunnar and taking off her heavy coat inside the house. She had been in the kitchen the last time she was there and tried to remember where everything was. She started talking as she made the hot chocolate.

"What have you two boys been up to?"

"Just taking care of the livestock," said Coy, "How about you?"

"You know, basketball games, Christmas dance, just stuff like that."

Gunnar looked over to his dad who just stood there and looked back at him.

"Sounds like you've been busy," said Gunnar.

"Well a girl has to be social you know." Coy was starting to catch on. She poured the hot chocolate into three large mugs and they all went and sat around the large dining room table.

"Coy," she said, "I'm here to teach Gunnar to dance."

The men looked at each other, then Coy said, "Son I'm going outside."

He didn't touch his hot chocolate. Coy stayed out as long as he could. He couldn't feel his face, so he knew it was time. He stomped his feet several times to let them know he was coming in. He could already hear the music playing loud.

He walked in to find the kids holding hands and dancing to a fast song.

"I'm dancing!" Gunnar yelled out.

"I can see," Coy yelled back over the loud music.

Still dancing with Gunnar, she asked, "Coy do you now see any reason Gunnar can have for not asking me to go to the Valentine's Dance?"

"No, I can't," said Coy.

"All right," said Gunnar, "Will you go to the Valentine's Dance with me?"

"Maybe," she said. Gunnar stopped dancing and just stared at her. "Of course, I'll go with you, now start dancing again."

A slow song had come on the radio. She held him close and said, "See, this is how it's done."

Coy went over, grabbed a newspaper and sat

on the couch with his back to the kids.

The song ended and Jesse said, "That's all for today's dancing lesson. I'd better get packed up and go home." Before she left, she grabbed both of Coy's hands.

"It is so good to see you smile and laugh again," she said. Jesse then pulled Gunnar towards the front door.

They had a good time at the Valentine's Dance even though Bill the captain of the basketball team asked Jesse to dance and she accepted. Gunnar danced once with Beth and once with Susan James, who all but left her body's imprint on him. Jesse was bothered by that and brought it up on the way home.

"I didn't hold her that close, she just enveloped me," he said.

"You sure didn't push her away."

"No, I try not to be rude."

He didn't get anywhere close to a goodnight kiss. In fact, she got out of his truck, yelled goodnight and walked to her door. He was on the highway headed home when he saw their neighbor, Mrs. Jenkins, just off the side of the road with a flat tire.

Coy woke up to a phone ringing. He looked at the clock in his room and it read 2:35. He got to the phone and said hello. Dave, the Chief of Police, was on the other end telling him there had been a bad accident and he should get to the Raton hospital as quick as he could.

Coy was trying to make sense of the conversation and asked who was involved.

Dave said Gunnar had been hurt bad. Coy

looked back to Gunnar's bedroom and said, "Okay, I'll be right there." He ran down the hall and turned on the light in Gunnar's room. He wasn't there.

Coy ran into the Emergency Room of the hospital and told the first nurse he saw he was Gunnar Danewood's father and asked where he was. The woman looked at him for a moment then said, "Follow me."

She walked quickly down to the Intensive Care Unit and told another nurse who he was. That nurse told him he needed to talk to the doctor that was caring for Gunnar and went into the ICU ward with Coy following.

"Doctor," she called out when they were close. "This is Mr. Danewood's father."

The doctor looked at Coy and said, "Your son was struck by a pickup truck and is in critical condition. He took a terrible impact. We have him on life support. Brace yourself, this will be hard to see."

When Coy saw Gunnar all wrapped up in gauze with blood oozing out, he felt his strength fall away and he started to fall. The doctor caught him and called for a chair. They got him in a chair and the doctor gave him a minute.

"Are you okay now?" he asked.

Coy slowly looked up and said, "Yes, I think so."

"The machines are keeping him alive currently. We will monitor him for 24 hours and watch for change. The impact was brutal, I'm afraid there isn't much hope."

Coy could only move his head slowly to bring things into focus. What had happened? Was this real? Was he really here in the hospital?

The head nurse told him he had to wait in the waiting room, but he could come in for fifteen minutes once an hour. He walked out into the waiting room and sat down in a chair. For some reason he looked at his hands. He hadn't even tried to touch or hold Gunnar. Then he remembered that he was oozing blood.

He sat there and thought of all the things they had done together and the plans he had for his son. Then he tried to remember the last time he told him he loved him. He couldn't remember. He felt the silent tears run off his face and fall to the floor. He was able to go in and sit by him five more times before Darlene came into the waiting room.

She sat down next to him and took his hand in hers. Tears rolled down her face as she said, "I am so sorry."

He turned and looked at her as if she wasn't there. She leaned back shocked by the vacant look out of his eyes. He didn't speak, he just looked back down at the floor.

Coy looked up at the clock on the wall. "I can go in now," he said.

Then he walked through the door into the ICU ward. Spider walked in when Coy was in with Gunnar.

"How's Gunnar?" he asked.

"They tell us he's critical, he's on life support. I am worried about Coy, his eyes are vacant."

"I'll go in with him next time, maybe that will help."

"They say only one person is allowed at a time."

"Yeah right," said Spider.

When Coy came out, Spider didn't hesitate. He walked up, hugged Coy hard and asked him, "How're you doing Coy?"

That did it, being hugged by his older friend. Coy began to cry and try to talk.

"He just lays there. He doesn't move or talk. I get right next to him, but I can't reach him. He's slipping away and I can't reach him." Then Coy really began to cry hard. Spider helped him into a chair still holding him. Coy started to pull it together after a few minutes.

Spider made eye contact with Darlene and said, "Hon, would you get me a milkshake? I missed breakfast." He held up two fingers.

She caught his meaning and said, "Sure, I'll be right back."

She came back with three.

"Here Coy, drink that," said Spider, "It will do you good."

Coy looked at it like he didn't know what it was at first. Spider gently pushed it up to his mouth and said, "They taste good at times like these."

Coy did what his friend told him to do. Getting something in his stomach seemed to help him. Darlene caught it right away. He was coming back and moving better.

"I'll go in with you next time," said Spider.

"They say only one person is allowed in at a time," said Coy.

"Yeah, well, we'll see about that," said Spider winking at Coy.

Darlene was so relieved to see Coy smile just a little and nod his head. When Coy and Spider came out from seeing Gunnar, they were sad and quiet as they sat down in the chairs.

"Has anyone told you what happened?" asked Coy.

Spider looked over to Darlene then back to Coy. "No one has told you about the wreck yet?"

"No, I got the call to come here and have just been going in and sitting with him."

"Do you want to hear it here?" asked Spider.

"Yes, I think so," said Coy.

"Mrs. Jenkins was stopped out on the state highway with a flat tire. Gunnar was coming home after the school dance and saw her barely off the road trying to jack up her truck. He pulled up behind her and started helping her change the tire. A car coming from the south saw them by the side of the road and turned on his high beams. A pickup was coming in the opposite direction. The pickup headed south was blinded by the other car's headlights and didn't see Gunnar until it was too late. The driver has been charged with vehicular manslaughter. Mrs. Jenkins said he pushed her away, just as the pickup hit him. He saved her life," he said softly.

Coy leaned over in his chair and cried silently. Shaking his head, he said, "Why, why do these things happen?"

"I don't know Coy, I just don't know," said Spider.

"He saved her life and lost his."

"He did, he sure did," said Spider, watching Coy slowly shake his head.

CHAPTER 15

It's Time

Spider went in and asked to speak to Gunnar's doctor. He stood there and thought for a moment before turning and walking back. He nodded to Darlene before he started speaking to Coy.

"Coy you need to go home, take a shower and take a nap if you can. I'll stay here until you get back. I'll call you if there is any change," he said.

"I don't know," said Coy, "it seems like I should stay here."

"You look pretty rough. It's time for you to go home and get cleaned up."

"I haven't thought about that. I guess you're right,"

"I'll be right here. Darlene you go with him and get him to eat something before you guys come back."

"Okay," she said, standing.

Her standing prompted Coy to stand. She wrapped her arm in his and started walking. He was almost like a small child being told what to do by others. She got him home and in the shower. Then she called Spider on his cell phone. Spider told her the doctor said decisions would have to be made soon. She told him she understood, hung up the phone and cried silent tears.

She went into a bathroom and washed her face. She had ham sandwiches with chips on paper plates ready, when he came into the living room.

"I'm not hungry," he said.

"Neither am I, but Spider told me to feed you and I better do what he says," she said smiling.

"Yeah, I guess that's right," he said coming over.

After they ate, she got him to lay down on the couch. She sat by his head and told him to close his eyes. She gently stroked his hair at his temples. He was so exhausted he fell asleep immediately.

He woke with a start three hours later. Him waking woke her.

"What time is it?" he asked sitting up. She yawned and found a clock.

"It's four in the afternoon."

"We better get back to the hospital," he said.

"Yes, I'm sure there is no change or Spider would have called, but we should go back."

She could see the difference in him. He was concerned and talking fast, but his eyes looked like he was thinking clearly.

Spider stood when they walked in. "I have been in four times, there is no change. You look better, you must have eaten something."

"Darlene makes a mean ham sandwich," he said.

"I really need to go check on the boys at the ranch. You two stay here. I'll be back tonight sometime and Darlene you get him to eat supper tonight."

"Check in on Jesse," said Darlene.

Spider smiled. "Like always," he said.

They settled in to wait and Darlene said, "Maybe you should talk to Gunnar." Coy looked up. "You know, say what you feel, maybe say the hard things that people should say but don't."

He looked back down. "Yeah, the hard things," he said.

The next time he came out it was obvious he had been crying. He fell into a chair and after a couple of deep breaths said, "I did what you said. I said all the things I should have told him every day. I told how good he was and how much I need and love him. I didn't do that enough."

She reached over and took his hand. "None of us do," she said.

Coy went in every hour and Darlene went in every other time with him. The nurses raised their eyebrows but let it happen. Spider came back at 8:30 that night.

"I just ate a hamburger and large order of fries at the cafe," he said. "Man, that hit the spot. Have you got him to eat supper tonight?"

"Not yet," she said.

"You two go down and get something at the cafeteria, I'll stay here."

"You heard the man," said Darlene.

"I'll go, but I doubt I can eat much," said Coy.

She got him to eat most of a tuna sandwich and about half of her French fries. They walked back in the waiting room holding hands. They had only sat there for ten minutes when Coy said, "I can go back in now."

Spider watched the door as he talked to make sure Coy didn't come back out. "It's getting close to twenty-four hours with no change. Sometime within the next twelve hours they will come to Coy and ask about taking Gunnar off life support. That's why I wanted him eating and sleeping. He is going to need us right beside him at that time. If you need to go see Jesse now might be a good time."

"I'll tell him where I'm going before I leave. Spider you have always done things like this for me and others. You are such a good person."

"Me? I'm just a rough old cob of a cowboy."

"Yeah right," she said patting his hand.

Darlene stood when Coy came out. "I need to go check in with Jesse. I should be back in an hour or so."

"I understand," he said.

She hadn't been gone fifteen minutes when Coy stood up quickly. "I haven't fed the cattle!" he said.

"Sit down and relax. The boys from the ranch have been looking after your cattle and horses. They even offered to do it without being told to. They might be better hands than I thought."

"I'll try to make it right with them when this is over," he said. "Over," he said again. "What if Gunnar doesn't respond, what if he just stays like this?"

"Then there will come a time when decisions have to be made. Coy, I'll stand with you if that happens. No matter what you decide, I'll stand with you."

Spider could see the weight of what was coming bearing down on Coy. He went in with him during his next visit and stood beside him. Darlene came back and Spider went home for the night. He was there at six the next morning. Gunnar's doctor asked to see him at 7:30. Spider watched, it was a big effort for Coy to stand.

"I'll go with you," said Spider.

In a small office the doctor explained that it was now over thirty-six hours after the accident and Gunnar showed no change. "It's time for some difficult decisions," he said. Coy nodded his head. "There are people here I would like you to talk to that are experienced in some of these situations." Coy raised his head and looked at the doctor. "In most situations like this they have been very helpful."

Spider knew what was coming and could tell Coy didn't. "It won't hurt to listen," he said, trying to be positive. The nurse gave Coy a room number. They told Darlene they would be back in a few minutes and started for the room. Spider was walking alongside of Coy when he stopped and looked at him.

"They want to tell me about donating organs, don't they," he said.

Spider moved where he was directly in front of Coy. "Yes, I think they will."

"They are going to tell me to take him off life support and donate his organs."

"No, I don't think they are going to say that. I think they are going to ask you to think about donating his organs, if there is no possibility that Gunnar can recover."

"I'm not pulling the plug on my son. I'm not going to do that!"

"Okay, what do you want to do, go back or listen to them?"

"There's no need to listen to them, I'm not going to do it."

"Then we need to go back to the waiting room."

"Maybe I'm being selfish, but I can't pull the plug on Gunnar."

"Okay," said Spider walking alongside of him going back to the waiting area.

Darlene stood when they came back. She could tell Coy was bothered about something. He finally said, "I'm going to see if I can go in now."

She looked over to Spider. He shook his

head a little, meaning don't ask.

When Coy was through the doors Spider said, "He is struggling even thinking about donating Gunnar's organs. Has Jesse said anything about wanting to see Coy?"

"Yes," said Darlene, "I told her that Coy needs time to be alone and she understood."

"Now might be a good time for him to see her. Seeing a young vibrant girl might help him make a decision."

"Okay, if you think it will help him, I'll call her right now," she said.

Coy had been in with Gunnar two more times when Jesse walked into the waiting area. He stood. She ran to him and hugged him. "I'm so sorry this happened," she said through her tears while hugging him. "I'm just so sorry."

Coy hugged her and kissed her on her hair. "I know Hon, I know," he said.

"How can this be? How can he be in there barely alive?" she asked.

"It just is Jesse, it just is," he said hugging her.

"I didn't kiss him goodnight after the dance," she said and looked down.

All three adults looked at her.

"I didn't like the way he danced with Susan James and told him. Now I wish I had just let it go. I would give anything to give him a kiss now."

"If he was here with us, he would tell you not to give it another thought. Those things happen when you're young," Coy said, still hugging her.

She stopped crying and apologized for it.

"There is no need to apologize, your mother and I have cried so much I doubt we have any tears left."

Everyone sat down. Jesse sat next to Coy. Darlene could see Coy look at Jesse with affection. She had been Gunnar's friend for a long time. She stayed with Spider when Coy and Darlene went in to see Gunnar the next time. She told Spider she wanted to see Gunnar.

"Do you trust my judgement?" he asked.

"Yes," she said.

"You need to remember him the way you knew him. He isn't there anymore. His body is in there being kept alive by machines, but Gunnar just isn't there anymore."

"There isn't any hope?"

"Not according to the doctor I talked to. It might be helpful to Coy if you told him you love him but need to go back to school, okay? He has a tough decision to make."

"About donating organs?"

"Exactly, I think seeing you healthy and so full of life might help him make a choice."

Coy came back in the room a few minutes after Spider and Jesse had talked. She stood and went to him.

"I need to go back to school. Give me another hug before I go. I love you so much. If you need me just call, okay?" she whispered to him.

He nodded and told her he loved her too. He watched her walk away. He watched her until she got on the elevator then sat down.

"What if it was Jesse that needed a heart, would you let her have Gunnar's?" asked Spider.

"I have been selfish," Coy said softly.

"What if Gunnar was able to speak? He gave up his life saving Mrs. Jenkins. How would he feel about giving part of his body to save other people?"

"You're right, I just don't know if I can do it."

"Have you thought about what he would want? Would he want to just linger there for weeks and finally die? The Gunnar I knew made things happen. Maybe it's time for you to help him make this happen."

"You're right, I just have to come up with enough nerve to do it."

"I'll stand with you Coy," said Darlene.

"I will too," said Spider standing up. "Let's all go talk to the folks in that room."

"I guess it's time," said Coy.

CHAPTER 16

How Do I Say Goodbye

The three of them walked out from the meeting quietly. Spider and Darlene waited for Coy to speak. They were almost back to the waiting room when he said, "I'll have to tell him what I am going to do. One thing keeps coming to mind, what if he can hear me? How would you feel hearing your loved ones are turning off your life support machines?"

"It would depend on the person I guess," said Spider. "Myself, I couldn't think of anything better than stopping the agony. For me and for my loved ones left behind."

"I haven't thought about that, what Gunnar would think about all of us staying here by his side," said Coy. "Like you, I know he wouldn't want us to stay here and cry for him. Just about every pore of my body says don't do it and yet I know it's the right thing to do."

"That was well put, Coy. Let's talk to his doctor one more time," said Spider.

Darlene let the men go in without her. It seemed like Spider had helped Coy more than anyone.

He looked like he was carrying the weight of the world when he came back to the waiting room. He sat down in a chair and speaking quietly said, "I agreed to let them do it. It could benefit over 100 people. They left it up to me to pick the time. If each of you want to go in and say goodbye, now would be a good time." She could see the small tears rolling down his face. He made no effort to wipe them away. "I'll go last," he said after a pause.

Darlene came forward and kissed the top of his head and said, "I'll go first."

Spider stayed with him. Neither of them said a word until Darlene came back. Spider hugged her while she cried. Coy heard her and remembered Spider's words of the ones left behind. He stood and hugged Darlene when she moved from Spider.

"I'll go now," said Spider. He took in a breath, pulled up his western belt and pants, then headed for the door.

"Are you all right?" Darlene asked after Spider left.

"No, I don't know if I will ever be right again. I feel completely empty."

She hugged him hard for a while.

Spider came out with red eyes about four minutes later.

Coy started nodding his head. "I have to tell him now and say goodbye. I'll be in there for a while." He stood and walked slowly to the door and went in.

He stood beside his son crying softly. "How do I say goodbye, Son? There is nothing in me that wants to say it. I want you here with me at home. We lost your mother and now I'm losing you." He stopped, blew his nose and wiped his eyes. "If you can hear me, I want you to know I love you so much. I don't know if I can go on without you." He paused and wiped his eyes again.

"Now for the hard part. They have shown me all the results that show no brain activity. They say there is no hope. They want permission to turn off life support and let you stop breathing. They have these waiting lists of people that are going to die if they don't get organ replacements. Some of them are teenagers like you. I'm going to let them do it, Gunnar. I don't want to, but I'm going to do it. I know if you were here,you would want it too." He walked forward, put his hand on Gunnar's chest and said, "Goodbye, Gunnar."

He sat down in a chair until he felt he could stand. He walked over to the nurse and said, "Tell the doctor they can have his organs. I signed the papers about an hour ago." Then he walked out completely drained of emotion.

Nobody asked what he said in the room.

They felt they knew. Coy was like he was at first. There was no light in his eyes, only sadness. Spider and Darlene helped him with the arrangements for the funeral and burial at the ranch. She stayed out there most of the daylight hours.

Five days went by and they had the funeral. Coy wanted it like Judith's. The same lady sang a song. Flowers covered the ground around the area that held the casket. The local preacher said a few words and gave Gunnar's eulogy. He ended his words by adding how Gunnar's last act on this earth was saving the life of his neighbor. Everyone sang the doxology.

Coy just stood there during the short service with Spider on one side and John Hull on the other. Darlene and Jesse stood slightly behind them. It was the largest funeral the valley had seen in a long time. Cars and pickups were parked clear out on the highway blocking one lane.

Coy had to sit down at the end to shake people's hands. Before it was over, he quit. He passed out when the men began to lower the casket into the grave. The funeral director had smelling salts that brought him back around.

He looked at the man and said, "I wish you had just let me go with him."

Spider and Darlene got him into the house. Spider could see she was watching Coy closely. She got him over to one side and said, "I'm staying here until he gets better. We can't leave him alone right now."

"I could do it," said Spider.

"Yes, but you don't want to marry him like I do," she said.

Spider smiled. "You're right about that Hon. I'll go on and take care of Jesse and the ranch. The boys will probably be over about lunch time to check on his stock."

Darlene stayed with him and took care of him for the next twelve days. Coy wouldn't hardly eat and most of the time sat looking at the floor. She slept on the couch. Spider came over on the thirteenth morning and told Coy he thought the fence was down on the back side of the BLM ground and Coy's cows were getting over into the McDaniels' cattle. It took a minute for that to soak in. Coy stood and asked where at. Spider said he didn't know for sure but thought it was up high by the rock bluff.

"You better go put on some warm clothes. I brought my horse. Which one do you want me to put a saddle on?" asked Spider.

"The buckskin, yeah, saddle up the buckskin for me," he said going back to his bedroom.

Darlene watched him walk down the hall and turned to Spider with a thumbs up. He grinned and went outside. Coy came out wearing his insulated bibs and a heavy coat.

"This will probably take a while especially if many of the cows are mixed up," he said.

"Just be careful," said Darlene.

He nodded and left. She watched out the windows and saw Spider pointing to something up in the hills.

They were back by two that afternoon. They came in talking.

"That's what Tom said. He told me this morning he saw them on our side up by the rock bluff."

"Did you see any hair on the wire?" asked Coy.

"No, I didn't, but you know as well as I do a cow can crawl back through a fence," said Spider.

"Yeah but nothing was separated from its mother and I didn't hear any cows bawling up there."

"Well don't get mad at me, I was just trying to help."

"Yeah okay, I'm sorry. You want to stay for lunch?"

"That depends, what do you have?"

"What, are you getting picky about what you eat?"

"Maybe, you didn't answer, what have you got?"

"I swear, Darlene fix Mister Picky something to eat. I'm going to go wash my hands."

Coy walked down the hall and Darlene went to Spider and hugged him.

"Thank you, that's more than he's said this whole time."

Spider stayed and ate. He talked about the weather and asked if Coy had enough hay to make it through till spring. Coy ate and talked with Spider and Darlene. He went out that evening and checked the hay in his barn. Darlene could see him starting to come around.

Spider was back in ten days telling Coy they needed to check the back fence on the far west end that Billy used to own. Coy just looked at him.

"If you want me to ride up there and look the fences over that's okay, but don't lie about cattle being out."

"Don't get mad at me, I'm just here trying to help," said Spider.

"Yeah and after your help I end up in the saddle for almost four hours."

"You getting to old to check your own fences?" asked Spider.

"You lie like a rug, Spider. I'll go get my gear."

"Want me to saddle your horse?"

"I believe I can handle that."

Spider grinned at Darlene and said, "Okay, okay,"

When they came in that time, Coy seemed much better. He was on Spider about telling the same stories.

"I know I heard that one about the dog bringing the hammer back at least two times," said Coy.

"Then you heard it from someone else because I would have remembered telling you."

"Evidently not," said Coy.

"So now you're a critic of my story telling?"

"Somebody should be," said Coy.

"Are you going to eat with us today?" Coy asked smiling and waiting.

"Maybe."

"I knew it, I knew it. You just have to have the last word, don't you?"

Spider took a minute to answer. "Yes, Mister

Danewood, I'll eat with you."

Coy started laughing and went down the hall.

"He's doing much better today." said Spider. Darlene nodded and started an early supper.

Coy smiled that day as they ate. Spider mentioned Billy and Coy seemed to be in a good mood talking about him. Darlene picked up on that. Before Spider left Coy told him to thank the ranch hands for feeding his cows but he would take over now. Spider said okay, thanked Darlene for the meal and left. Later that evening, after watching television, Coy said he was going to go to bed. Darlene asked if they could watch the tape of him and Billy again. He said sure and put it on. When it was over, he put it up and said, "Now I am going to bed."

He had just gotten comfortable in his bed when the door opened, and Darlene came in. He raised up and asked, "What's the matter?"

"Nothing," she said getting into bed with him. She came to him and pressed her naked body against him. Her body was so warm it felt hot.

"Darlene, I don't know if I can do this," he said.

"Don't worry, I know you can, just relax and it will be okay."

Then she was kissing him. He relaxed and let it happen. Maybe it was the love making or the tension release, but whatever it was, Coy slept for almost nine hours. He woke to an empty bed. He used the bathroom and went looking for her. She was cooking breakfast in the kitchen.

"Good morning, Sugar," she said coming over to him.

"Don't start calling me Sugar," he said.

"How come?"

"It doesn't sound all that manly."

"After last night I don't think you have to worry about being manly."

"When we are out in public you have to call me Coy, okay?"

"After last night I'll call you anything you want, Sugar."

"You need to know I'm not ready to think about marriage."

"I didn't bring that up, you did. Let's just take this one step at a time."

"Last night was very special for me," he said.

"It was for me too, but I'll be going home today."

"Do you have to?"

"Yes, you are better now. I have a house and ranch to take care of and so do you."

"I'll miss you."

"That was the plan, Sugar," she said bringing their breakfast to the table smiling

CHAPTER 17

Graduation

L ife began to fall back into place for Coy. It seemed to him he was back where he started. He was alone with a big house and a ranch. The difference was Darlene and her family. She came over about once a week and brought lunch for them. Several times, they ate on the front porch and enjoyed a quiet time together.

In mid-May, Spider offered to come over and help gather his cattle and run them through the chute. Darlene and Jesse showed up at 1:00 with food. The men told them they only needed another forty minutes to finish, so the girls waited. The men opened the gates when they were finished and let the cattle out and came up to the house.

Darlene, being raised on a ranch, had a five-gallon bucket of water, soap and a towel waiting.

Spider washed up first and flung water droplets on Coy.

"That's about right," Coy said laughing.

"Wouldn't want to disappoint you," said Spider. "Now what's for lunch?"

"Homemade ham sandwiches and chips," said Jesse.

"Let me at it," said Spider.

"He's full of manners, isn't he," said Coy.

"Sometimes," said Darlene coming to his rescue.

After lunch, Jesse asked if she could go look in Gunnar's room. It shocked Coy. After he thought about it for a while, he said sure. She was in there for over ten minutes then came back outside.

"What's that letter in there on his dresser?" she asked.

"That's a letter his mother left for him to open on his 18th birthday."

"Are you going to open it?"

Darlene glanced over at her.

"It's okay," Coy said putting his hand on her shoulder. "Yes, I am going to open it on his birthday."

"Oh," said Jesse looking down.

They had a relaxing meal and sat on the porch for over an hour just visiting, then Spider stood.

"I guess we better get back to the ranch," he

said.

Everyone stood up and began packing the food that was left.

"Thanks for the help and for the food. Today was good," said Coy.

"Thanks for having us," said Darlene, before coming over and kissing him in front of everyone.

"Well, now I see why mom comes over here all the time," said Jesse.

Darlene told her to take the truck they came in. She would have Coy bring her home. Jesse said okay and took the leftover food with her and left.

Before Spider left, he told Coy the ranch had bought twelve roping steers and asked him to come over and rope with him.

"What day?" asked Coy.

"Wednesdays," said Spider, knowing that was the day Darlene went over to Coy's place.

Coy looked over to Darlene. She was grinning.

"How about Thursdays?" asked Coy still looking at her.

"I guess we can handle that," said Spider, with a big grin as he pulled out.

"I need to talk to you about Jesse," said Darlene.

"Okay," said Coy.

"She's not happy like she used to be. She hasn't gone to one school activity since Gunnar passed. She keeps up a good front, but I think she is really depressed."

"What can I do, or what can we do?"

"I can't come up with anything but a big change. You know something that she hasn't thought about, but something she would really like. I think going somewhere would help. I'm thinking of buying her tuition at an acting college in California. I think that new people and studying what she enjoys might be a big help. I would like to hear your thoughts on this."

"Wow, talking about taking me off guard. Well, California sure would be a change from here. She did like acting in the school play. What if she doesn't want to go?"

"Then she won't go. I'm not forcing her to go, I'm only offering it to her for a graduation present."

"Just surprise her with it and see if she wants it?" he asked.

"Exactly."

"The truth is I don't want her to leave. I love being around her, but for her mental health and maturing this might be the right thing to do. We do have to let our kids go sometime. The more I talk about it, the better it sounds. If she doesn't want to go, she can stay here. She can always come home, if things turn south."

He took Darlene home and drove back. Coy was alone again, but it wasn't as bad as before because now he had friends that came over.

He went over and talked to Gunnar's grave about Jesse.

Coy roped over at the McDaniels Ranch every Thursday unless it rained. The only time Darlene didn't come on Wednesdays was when they had a date later in the week. Coy saw Spider at the cafe for lunch at least three times a week.

Haying time was coming and before that graduation. Coy went over early one Thursday and found Darlene and Spider at the house. He proposed a plan of them loaning him a man to help put up his hay and then he would work the same hours for them putting up their hay.

"You don't have to do that," Darlene said softly.

"Oh yes I do," he said.

"He's come up with a good plan. We usually hire a few extra hands any way for haying season," said Spider. "I don't know how hard he'll work, but it sounds okay."

"How hard I'll work," said Coy. He started in on how Spider wouldn't know hard work if it bit him in the butt. Then he saw him wink at Darlene.

"You are a piece of work Spider," he said.

"Yeah, I guess," said Spider standing up and extending his hand. "Do we have a deal? You work for us the same hours as our man works for you?"

"Yes, we have a deal," said Coy, shaking his friend's hand.

"Good, let's go rope some steers."

Coy looked over to Darlene. She was smiling and shaking her head.

Everyone got dressed up for Jesse's graduation from High School. Darlene was nervous and Coy could see it.

"I just hope I'm doing the right thing," she

said.

"You are, let her make her decision and you will see," said Coy.

Darlene moved a lot in her chair but made it through the ceremony. Spider looked over at her. They found Jesse talking with a few of her friends after the graduates had marched out. Coy saw what Darlene tried to explain. Instead of being wildly happy, Jesse seemed subdued. They walked up to her.

"Congratulations," said Coy, "You made it!"

She smiled at him then came forward and hugged him.

"Got one of those for an old man?" Spider asked.

"You bet," she said and hugged Spider too.

"I have something for you, if you want it," said Darlene. "I mean I bought you a gift, but it is up to you if you decide to use it."

Jesse was having a hard time understanding.

Darlene handed her the airline ticket and said "This is a ticket to California. I have paid the tuition for the first year at Pepperdine College in Malibu. They offer two degrees in acting. Several famous actors have graduated from there."

They watched her eyes get big. She looked down at the ticket then up at her mom. She jumped forward and hugged her hard.

"Thank you, mom, thank you!" she yelled.

Her friends gathered around and she told them what her mother had just given her. Darlene looked over to Coy and he nodded while smiling.

Darlene cried by herself several times the next week as Jesse packed up. Her little girl was moving out. It had worked, Jesse was happy and enthusiastic again. Darlene knew it was for the best, but it still hurt. Coy tried to comfort her all he could. They drove her down to the airport at Albuquerque. Spider and Coy sat in the front, Darlene and Jesse in the back. Coy saw tears fill Jesse's eyes seeing her mother cry when they announced her flight.

"I'll call as often as I can," she said after hugging her mother for the last time. She looked back and saw Coy hug Darlene as she cried. Jesse waved and walked out of sight.

CHAPTER 18

Haying Time

They had agreed to start haying at Coy's place first, but he was still surprised when Spider drove the big tractor and baler in his drive. It was so much larger and more powerful than his.

"Thought we would bring our stuff over and speed things up a little," said Spider.

"I've got my equipment all greased up and ready," said Coy.

"You're going to be driving this on our fields, so you might as well get used to it here. It will allow you to put up you hay a lot faster."

"Not much doubt about that," said Coy. He thought about saying more, but let it go.

After the first two days, Coy was glad Spider

had brought the equipment over. He had made a few mistakes with it and was glad Spider wasn't there to see them. They finished his place in six days, faster than he had ever finished before. He was used to the equipment by then and helped them move it back to the McDaniels Ranch.

Coy finished his six days and stayed on working for Spider. He slept at home and took care of his stock early then drove over and started in running the baler. Darlene brought lunch out to the hands every day. They were finishing up on the twenty eight day after lunch, when Spider drove up and motioned for Coy to stop raking the hay. Spider had a man with him in the truck. Coy stopped the tractor and walked over to the two of them that had stepped out of the truck.

"I'm glad we moved you over to raking instead of baling," said Spider. "Your bales look worse than a dead thirty-dollar goat's butt."

Shaking his head, Coy said, "There's nothing wrong with my bales, but I'm curious, have you seen a lot of dead thirty-dollar goat butts?"

"No, but if you've seen one that's too many."

The other hand walked away laughing and shaking his head.

"Spider, I swear, I've known you all my life, but sometimes you still amaze me. Where do you come up with this stuff?"

"I'm a poet," he said.

The hired hand took out his handkerchief and wiped his eyes laughing harder.

"A poet?"

"Yeah I'm a ranch poet."

"Mister ranch poet can I get back to raking hay now?"

"Nope, Tom is going to take over for you and you are going to come with me."

Spider drove up on a hill that overlooked most of the hay fields and parked the truck.

"Heard anything new from Jesse?" he asked.

"No, I think Darlene read her last letter to you," said Coy.

"I've enjoyed you working with us in the hay. If you were polite, I might offer you a fulltime job."

"I've had fun working with the hands, but I think I'll just go back to running my place," said Coy.

"If you were to come back full time, I'd have to cut your wages on account of your age though."

"My age, what about you, you're old enough to be my dad."

"Be nice and respect your elders Coy."

"My age, my word I'm only forty."

"I have been waiting to tell you something until you were over the loss of Gunnar. This is tough stuff, but I think you deserve to know."

"Okay," said Coy.

"The night Judith died, I walked up to the big house to ask for some time off. I was sad and walking quietly. I got inside and clear down the hall before I heard Adam on the phone. He was talking to someone about a job. I heard him say, 'She just died, and they will be distracted.' He was hiring some men to kill you and Gunnar."

Coy leaned forward with wide open eyes.

"He told them they dropped the ball on the truck accident, but if they did a clean job like at the railroad crossing, he would pay them double. He told them he was going to Taos but would call from a casino in Durango and give them the go ahead. It took me a second to realize what I had heard. I walked out and went to my place to think. I went over the words I heard until I was sure. Adam McDaniels was responsible for your parents' death, your accident and almost your death."

Coy lowered his head and sat there.

"I wanted to tell you because it seemed to me, he got away with it. You are the one he hurt the most and didn't know."

Coy looked out his window and shook his head. "All for money. He killed my parents and tried to kill me all for money."

"And land," said Spider. "You and I are the only ones who know what he said that night, and I need to ask you to keep it that way. Darlene never knew anything about it, and shouldn't be held accountable for her father's actions."

"He was killed that night," said Coy.

"Yes, he was, before he could pay the men to kill you and Gunnar." Spider looked away for a moment then back to Coy.

"You and I will never speak of this again," he said.

"Agreed," Coy said quietly.

"Well, I guess if you're through working here

I'd better get you to your truck."

"Yes," said Coy, still thinking about what he had heard.

CHAPTER 19

Where It All Began

C oy was quiet for the next two weeks. Darlene got tired of it and asked him about it. He told her sometimes the past just seemed to come forward and bother him. He told her he was sure it would pass. He made up his mind after he said those words, that he wouldn't let Adam McDaniels affect him ever again. He vowed to go forward and not backwards.

Coy and Darlene continued to see each other as often as they could. She noticed he was getting more affectionate and holding her more. Mid October she started leaving Wednesday nights after their lovemaking rather than spending the night there. He would hold her and try every way he could to get her to stay, but she always had something to do the next morning.

Coy opened Judith's letter to Gunnar on Sunday the tenth day of November. He was surprised to find a smaller envelope inside with instructions to give it to Coy. It was a shock. He took it out to the front porch, sat in a chair and opened it. There was a slight breeze as he read.

It's been a year now and you should be over forty. That is still too young to live alone. I imagine you have been dating Darlene for a while. Don't be so surprised, I saw it twice. Once when she came to see you in the hospital that you never knew about. The other time I went to see her about that visit. When she saw me, she only had concern on her face that something else had happened to you. I knew then how much she cared for you. Coy, I know how much you loved me, but the truth is you always had a soft spot for Darlene, and I knew it. We would talk about how bad she acted but you wouldn't ever say how much you disliked her. I knew it then and I know it now. It was and is okay. You gave me all the love you had but now I am gone. Now it's time to give all your love to another. Kind of surprised you didn't I.

Goodbye Sweetheart,
Judith

Coy let his hands fall to his sides still holding the letter. "My word," he said. He sat there and looked up to the hill where the graves were.

Had he failed her somehow all those years? She said he hadn't.

Was she just being nice? *No*, he thought, *she wasn't like that. She always said what she felt.* He smiled a little thinking of some of their "talks" as she called them. No, if she felt he had acted wrong she would have let him know. The letter said it all very clear. He thought back to their talk on the hill and remembered her making him nod his head that he understood. She was now reaffirming those words for him.

He went up to her grave and thanked her for the letter and told her he needed it somehow. He told her he probably wouldn't be back to talk to her, that it was time to move forward. He felt relieved walking back to the house. It was time to look ahead not behind.

He called Darlene that night. She asked after a few words what was wrong. He told her nothing, he just wanted to hear her voice. She asked if she needed to come over.

"I would never turn that down, but you don't have to. It's late and you need to get some sleep.   Good night, I love you Darlene," he said.

She pulled both arms to her chest. "I love you too Coy, goodnight," she said, and gently put down the phone. That was the first time he said he loved her since they were kids. Little tears ran down her face, but she didn't care, her heart was warm.

Coy called Darlene late the next morning and asked if she would meet him up on the mountain by the rock bluff at noon the next day. She was surprised but said yes and asked if he wanted her to pack a lunch. He said that would be great.

He hadn't asked her to ride a horse up there, but that was the way they had met before, so she rode a horse up to the bluff. She spread out her blanket and waited. He rode up in a new western shirt, a leather coat and a new black cowboy hat. She was impressed and went to the fence. Holding the wires apart, she said, "You didn't say I should dress up."

"You look wonderful, did you bring a blanket?"

"Yes, it's under the bluff."

"Let's go sit down," he said.

"It's pretty up here," he said, after they had sat for a little bit.

"Yes, it is," she said watching his movements.

He moved around until he was right in front of her. "Just look at you. You don't seem to age. You're so pretty," he said. She lowered her head, but he reached over and gently lifted it back up.

"Don't look down, not today. This is where it all started, here under this bluff."

"It really started when we were dating," she said.

"Yes, you're right, it did. I tried to make you stay away, but something always seemed to draw us back together."

The wind blew some of her hair into her face. He reached up and gently moved it away and over to the side.

"I don't know for sure when I started loving you or even if I never stopped. These last few weeks ,when you left at night, my heart feels as empty as the house. I never want to see you leave again. Darlene, I love you."

He had a little trouble getting it out of his leather coat pocket, but finally brought out a little black box and opened it. There was a small diamond ring.

"Darlene, will you marry me?" he asked.

Tears were running down her face as she nodded her head yes.

"Yes Coy, I'll marry you." She wiped her tears away and said, "You have always been so kind and caring to Jesse and me, I hope you will be as nice to our next child as you are to her."

"I will do my best, but right now let me put this ring on your finger," he said.

She stopped crying as he put it on and was watching him.

"You don't understand," she said. "I said as nice to our next child."

"Yes," he said nodding his head.

She leaned forward and put the palm of her hand on the side of his face.

"In a little over six months I'm going to have our baby."

The shock hit Coy clear down to his toes.

"You mean you're pregnant?"

"Yes, that's why I have been leaving your house at night. I'm sick almost every morning."

She could see the joy all over his face. He came forward and hugged her so hard she had to ask him to let up.

"A baby, our baby," he said. Then he became concerned. "Is it safe for you, I mean at our age?"

"Yes, I have been going to an obstetrician and she says if I do as she says the baby and I will be fine."

Coy hugged her again, but this time like she was made of glass. She had to smile.

Coy couldn't believe how his life had come back together. He was going to hold his own child. Finally, after all the loss and tragedies of the early years, life was starting again.

THE END

Incarceration

Book 3

CHAPTER 1

Sick Every Morning

Winter gave way to spring and Coy was at his ranch driving the ten-year-old flatbed truck he carried round bales on when something blew-up under the hood. He turned the key off and looked at the gauges. It had overheated.

He got out, lifted the hood and saw the top radiator hose had blown. He thought about it for a minute, then started walking back to the house. More than likely the thermostat had stuck not allowing the antifreeze to get to the radiator.

It had been a good old truck and never given him any trouble until today. He got to the house and called Darlene, told her what had happened, and asked her to tell Spider he would need several hours to repair the truck. He drove into town to the Napa Auto Parts store. He was signing the charge receipt when he heard a voice behind him.

"Hello Coy," it said.

He turned and saw Phil, his longtime friend, and owner of the local feed store. He hadn't seen Phil since he and Darlene were married.

"Phil," he said, "It's good to see you."

"Looks like you have had some truck trouble," said Phil.

"Yeah, my old flatbed overheated and blew a radiator hose."

"You think the thermostat stuck?" asked Phil.

"More than likely," said Coy, "I bought one just in case."

"Here," said Phil, "I'll carry the antifreeze out for you. I need to talk to you anyway."

Outside, standing by the McDaniels Ranch pickup, Phil said, "My wife is kind of heartbroken."

"How come?" asked Coy.

"She thinks she, or I have done something to offend you and you never come in the store anymore."

"No," said Coy, shaking his head. "I've just been busy, that's all. I was really down after Gunnar passed, then I married Darlene. Now she's pregnant and sick every morning. I'm trying to learn how to run the McDaniels spread and keep mine going at the same time."

"I've told her it was something like that, but she won't listen. Could you stop by the store and say hello to her?"

"Sure, sure I will," said Coy.

"Thanks, it will really cheer her up. I'll see you later," he said then went back inside the parts house.

Coy climbed into the pickup and thought. He couldn't remember the last time he was in Phil's feed store. The McDaniels Ranch had their feed delivered in big trucks from a wholesaler up in Trinity Colorado. He used that feed for his stock and was paying the ranch back once a month. He'd better go see his dear old friend, Jean.

There were no customers in the store. Jean saw him and came around from behind the counter.

"Coy," she said, before walking up and hugging him tightly.

"Jean, I'm sorry for not being around. I've been covered up taking care of my place and learning how the McDaniels Ranch runs." Then he looked around and noticed the shelves were only about half full.

"I thought we offended you in some way," she said.

"No, not at all, what's happened? How come the shelves aren't full?"

"It's just business," she said. "The big farm store up in Trinity has started calling on ranchers down here and delivering feed at the same price we sell it for here. We can't blame people for paying the same price and having feed delivered. Times change Coy, they are one of over fifty stores and have better buying power than we do."

"Jean, I'm so sorry, I've been buying feed from them. I'm part of your problem."

"No, you're not, you could never be a problem to me," the older woman said.

"Is there any way you can do what they do?"

"We haven't talked about that," she said.

"Could you deliver feed to the local ranchers?"

"We hired Toby Jenkins to help load feed on the dock. I guess Phil or I could drive and have Toby unload."

"Okay, I'll be your first delivery," said Coy. "Bring out a thousand pounds of horse feed and a thousand pounds of cattle cubes when it's convenient and have Toby stack it in the feed room at the barn."

"You don't have to do this," she said.

"Maybe not, but I'm going to. Now I have to go fix my flat bed."

He kissed her on the side of her face and left. Coy stopped at two ranchers he knew on the way out to his place and told them that Phil now delivered feed and if people didn't start buying from them, Raton would lose its one and only feed store. Judging by their response, he thought the problem would solve itself.

He fixed his flatbed, filled it up with antifreeze, and got it going.

It was then 1:00 o'clock, so he stopped in the town cafe and ate lunch. He told two other ranchers there that the local feed store would now deliver and asked them to buy feed from Jean and Phil. Once they heard it might close, they agreed quickly. He drove back to the McDaniels Ranch. He explained the situation to Darlene and was shocked by her reaction.

"It's their fault," she said boldly. "That woman is grumpy and has never been nice to me. I don't think she likes me."

"Jean?" he asked surprised.

"Yes, Jean, Phil isn't overly friendly, but Jean has always been short with me. There is no way this ranch is going to buy feed from that rude woman," she said firmly.

They had been married for several months and he knew she wouldn't change her mind, so he let it go. He said okay and walked out the door. He stayed out until twilight.

That night at the dinner table she apologized for being so blunt then added, "She's been hateful to me since I was a teenager."

Coy just nodded his head and said, "Oh."

"I know she and Judith we're good friends."

"Is that what this is about?"

"No. Well, maybe."

"Are you jealous of her and Judith's friendship?"

"How can I not be? I've seen Jean and Judith hug each other with you standing there smiling. You never smile at me like that,"

"I'm not going to argue with you about this," he said. "I know you are pregnant and uncomfortable, but I'm not going to cut off my lifelong friends because you don't feel good. Darlene, I love you. If you don't get along with them, that's okay, I won't bring it up again. I've had a long day and I'm going to bed."

ABOUT THE AUTHOR

When a fire destroyed his milk barn in 1981, Paul was forced to find work off the farm. He rode with a veterinarian for a year and a half then moved on to artificially inseminating cattle. Because he had met so many ranchers and dairymen, he became a feed salesman and eventually got the opportunity to manage a feed store. He did these things while continuing to run some cattle on his own place.

He brings realistic situations and humor to his writings from people and places he has met along life's journey.